INVENTING THE VISCOUNT

THE BLUESTOCKING SCANDALS BOOK 2

ELLIE ST. CLAIR

Facebook: Ellie St. Clair

Cover by AJF Designs

Do you love historical romance? Receive access to a free ebook, as well as exclusive content such as giveaways, contests, freebies and advance notice of pre-orders through my mailing list!

Sign up here!

Also By Ellie St. Clair

The Bluestocking Scandals
Designs on a Duke
Inventing the Viscount
Discovering the Baron
The Valet Experiment
Writing the Rake
Risking the Detective
A Noble Excavation
A Gentleman of Mystery

The Bluestocking Scandals Box Set: Books 1-4
The Bluestocking Scandals Box Set: Books 5-8

For a full list of all of Ellie's books, please see
www.elliestclair.com/books.

CHAPTER 1

LONDON, 1820

*L*ady Fredericka Ashworth watched the man she had been supposed to marry waltz off with another woman.

His wife. And her new friend.

She wasn't the least bit jealous.

No, Valentine St. Vincent, Duke of Wyndham, was not the man for her. She had known it the moment she had met him, when she had seen his gaze slide past her and fall upon the woman he would eventually marry.

As it turned out, she and the duke wouldn't have particularly suited — though she would have married him anyway.

"Are you all right?"

Freddie turned her head to the voice of her friend, Miss Jemima St. Vincent, Valentine's sister. While Freddie and the duke did not develop a relationship, she had, at the very least, formed a great friendship with his sister.

"Perfectly fine," Freddie answered, her smile true. "I was

simply thinking about how well everything worked out. Had your brother and I married, he would have been miserable."

Jemima quirked an eyebrow.

"What makes you say that?"

"He is obviously a passionate man, and there was no spark between us. We would have been friends, but nothing more."

"Would *you* have been fine with that?"

"Yes, I would have," Freddie said with conviction, laughing at Jemima's surprised expression. "Friendship is much more than many are lucky enough to have. Besides, he is one of few men who would have likely put up with my... eccentricities."

"As he does with mine," Jemima murmured, and Freddie nodded.

"Exactly."

Jemima looked around them at her family's ballroom, filled with people who were eager to make the new duchess' acquaintance. Freddie and Jemima were currently hiding in the corner. Jemima's friend, Celeste Keswick, had reluctantly agreed to a dance orchestrated by her mother but would be returning shortly.

"But, Freddie, don't you want *more?*" Jemima asked, her plea impassioned. "Don't you desire love, like Rebecca and Val have found?"

Freddie adamantly shook her head.

"Not at all," she said, setting her chin. "I thought I had it once before. It wasn't worth it."

"Oh Freddie, I had no idea—"

But Freddie smiled sadly and shook her head.

"Another time. Suffice it to say that I would be content with a man who would respect me, be friendly to me, and allow me to do as I please."

"Not a particularly strong man, then?" Jemima asked, to which Freddie shrugged.

"I suppose you can say that."

"Must you marry at all?" Jemima persisted, to which Freddie nodded sadly.

"If I didn't have to, I wouldn't," she said. "But I am already four-and-twenty. My parents are desperate for me to marry. They will support me for as long as they must, of course, but I know they worry — and rightly so. My sisters are married, and with no brothers, one day my father's title will go to a cousin. I should hardly like to have to place the entirety of my existence on his benevolence — or lack thereof."

"It isn't fair, is it?" Jemima murmured, to which Freddie shook her head.

"Of course not. But that is the reality of our lives, Jemima, so we must make the best of it. Ah, here comes my mother now with a potential beau in tow. She was truly heartbroken when your brother and Rebecca married, you know."

Jemima squinted at the approaching pair. "Who is that with her? We haven't been part of society long enough for me to know many of the *ton* yet."

Freddie craned her neck around the dizzying array of swirling dancers before them. The man beside her mother was only slightly taller than she was, which meant he was rather short himself. Brown hair tinged with red, trepidation on his face...

"Oh! I'm in luck. It's simply Lord Gilmore."

"What of Lord Gilmore?" Celeste said as she rejoined them, her pale cheeks flushed from the exertion of dancing. "Please don't say my mother is bringing him here for me. I am finished with dancing this evening. Besides, he's nice enough, if a bit of a bore."

"Agreed," Freddie said with a smile. "But no, it is my mother this time. Our families have known one another for ages. There is nothing particularly disappointing to say about Miles except that he hardly ever speaks and conversing with him is akin to speaking to a statue."

"My brother likes him," Celeste said with a shrug. "I haven't heard many speak ill of him. An agreeable sort. Goes along with everything."

An idea sparked in Freddie's mind — one that Jemima clearly suspected by the intense way she was looking at her.

"You have a rather intriguing look on your face, Freddie," she remarked, and Freddie nodded. Perhaps they could all find what they were looking for — both Freddie, as well as her parents.

There was only one unknown factor.

Miles himself.

* * *

MILES FOLLOWED Lady Rothwell across the ballroom with trepidation. He had no wish to dance with her daughter, but the woman had been insistent. When Lady Rothwell wanted something, well, she was known to chase after it with the stubbornness of a dog after a stick.

When he finally realized that she wasn't going to let him alone without his agreement, he decided he would come and get this over with.

He knew she was chattering incessantly beside him as they walked, but he didn't bother attempting to determine just what she was saying, for he knew her well enough to be aware that her words flew so fast they required a great deal of concentration, and usually it wasn't worth the effort.

Lady Fredericka, on the other hand...

Despite her diminutive size, it was easy to find her through the crowd. She was as pleasing to the eye as she had always been. The same dark-brown hair, the color of cocoa, piled high on her head in the latest style, well-crafted ringlets floating around her temples. The same warm brown eyes, wide in her heart-shaped face. That same knowing, intelligent smile on her pink, bow-shaped lips.

A smile that was currently directed at him. Why did she look so cunning, so satisfied? It slightly unnerved him. He hadn't seen her in a couple of years now, for their paths didn't cross nearly as often as they had as children. He only attended these things to appease his mother, despite the fact that he hated them with all of his being.

The music was too loud, the ballrooms too echoey, and the conversation too difficult.

But his mother was insistent that they attend, that he begin the search for a wife. She was desperate for grand-children.

And he would do anything for his mother. Without her, who knows where he would be. Likely a madhouse. Instead, he was the Viscount of Gilmore, heir to the Marquess of Dorrington, and no one knew his secret.

He intended to keep it that way, but accompanying ladies such as Lady Fredericka in dances only added to the challenge. What made it worse was he knew her well enough to be aware that she wasn't an empty-headed simpering miss. No, Lady Fredericka was one of the most observant people he knew, and one of the very reasons he attempted to keep his distance from her, despite her beauty.

But here he was.

"Lady Fredericka," he said with a bow before holding out a hand. "Would you care to join me in a dance?"

He looked up at her, awaiting her response.

"Of course, Lord Gilmore," she said with a smile, placing her hand in his. He led her to the floor, saying nothing else, both relieved and chagrined when a waltz began to play. They were easiest to dance, for he only had to count, but if she decided to have a conversation, it might prove rather difficult.

But, of course, she did. She had always had much to say. He leaned back slightly to determine just exactly what she was now saying.

"How are you enjoying the Season?"

"Just fine," he responded, noticing from up close how much she had grown into her looks. She was still small, but he was struck by the warmth of her brown eyes and her easy smile. She had always been a precocious little thing, but now she had gentled somewhat. "It's been busy."

"I can imagine," she said, before saying something that he didn't quite catch.

"Pardon me?"

"I said that it is good to see you again. It has been so long."

"It has," he said, wishing she would dispense with the polite conversation and allow them to simply dance.

"I believe our fathers are still acquaintances, but it is a shame they do not spend time together as they used to," she said, to which Miles shook his head.

"It is not a shame, Lady Fredericka. You know as well as I do that my father has never been easy to get along with, and it has only worsened as he has aged."

Her eyes widened in shock and her mouth snapped shut. Thank goodness.

Unfortunately, it didn't last.

"How is your mother? She is always such a dear. I have seen her time and again when she comes for tea."

"My mother is well," he said, pleased she had finally found a topic of conversation which he was interested in taking part in. "She especially enjoys visits with your mother. A respite from her own home."

"Yes," she said, blinking but nodding sagely. "I suppose that is true."

"She always liked you, Lady Fredericka."

"Oh, come, Miles, call me Freddie, please. The fact that we have aged is hardly reason for us to become so formal with one another."

"Very well," he said, softening, but then muttered a curse as he stumbled slightly into Freddie when they both stepped forward at the same time. He had become distracted and stopped counting.

"I'm sorry," he apologized, but she shook her head, saying something he didn't quite catch before a smile softened her lips.

"You know, Miles, no one has regarded me so intensely for quite some time."

He swallowed. There was a reason he did so, and it wasn't the same one she had conjectured. She squeezed his hand, which was currently outstretched and wrapped around hers.

"Miles, I must ask you something. Something important."

He nodded.

"Would you— would you call upon me tomorrow?"

Miles lost count altogether at her question. He stopped, blinked, and she, continuing to move, ran right into him. He caught her, holding her up. Had he heard her correctly? She wanted *him* to call upon her? He asked her to repeat herself, which she did. Yes, it seemed he was correct.

"Why?" he said, causing her cheeks to flush beautifully, and then he moved her out of the way before another couple knocked into her.

"Why not?" she asked with a shrug before taking her plump bottom lip between her teeth, worrying it for a moment – causing an unexpected flicker of desire to course through him. "We have known one another long enough to be aware that there is nothing distasteful about the other, no family secrets or skeletons in the cupboard." Or so she thought. "Unless my mother is in the wrong, you require a

7

wife, so you are currently seeking one out, and I am far past the marrying age. I need someone to provide for me. Does that answer your question?"

If he was right, she seemed angry with him, though why, he had no idea. Her reasons for courting were as unromantic as he had ever heard, but perhaps she had a point.

"It's only a call," she said, holding her head high. "It is not as though I am proposing marriage. Yet."

Miles took her hand and led her off the dance floor, needing to be free of the swirling dancers, to go somewhere where he could properly hear her and not have her words garbled by the music.

"Freddie," he said when they were out of the ballroom and into the foyer to where the doors led. "Are you sure about this?"

A frown marred her perfect features.

"Do you not *want* to call upon me? I understand if you do not wish to. Perhaps there is someone else you are—"

"There is no one else."

"It was just a thought, Miles," she said, and he could tell she was attempting to feign nonchalance. "If you'd prefer not to, it is perfectly fine."

He sighed. She had clearly decided that something was the matter with *her*, which was so far from the truth. He was surprised by her lack of confidence.

"All right, Freddie. I'll be there."

"Well, you needn't be so excited about it. You know what — this was a terrible idea."

She moved to brush past, but he grasped her arm and gently turned her toward him.

"I will see you tomorrow," he said firmly. "Goodnight."

It was he who walked past her now. It was time to find his mother, and get the hell out of here.

CHAPTER 2

"*O*h, Miles, Lady Fredericka? How lovely! I never would have thought the two of you— Well, I suppose perhaps when you were younger it crossed my mind, but then..."

"Then you realized that she was too smart a woman to marry a man like me?"

"I'm sure, Miles, if she came to truly know you, she would love you as much as I do," his mother said, though she flushed guiltily as she sat on the window seat in her parlor, a cup of tea in her hand. Miles spent many mornings visiting with her. It had been one source of concern since he had taken his own rooms a few years past — leaving her here, alone with his father. But he trusted his brother enough to look after her, and he could not spend another night under the same roof as Lord Dorrington.

"She *is* rather astute," his mother said with a tinge of worry in her voice before taking a sip.

His mother was right. It was what had plagued Miles since that bloody dance with Freddie yesterday.

His mother's eyes were drawn to something behind him,

and Miles turned to find that the maids had entered with the rest of their breakfast. He nodded to them before they departed. It tortured him to no end that he often had to rely on his mother to keep up this ruse. But as a child, it had always been either that or being sent away and all but disinherited.

He preferred this.

"I think it will be fine," he said with a shrug. "As long as she doesn't speak too often from over my shoulder, and so long as I do not take her somewhere like Gunter's or a tea room, I should be able to hear her just fine. She speaks loudly and clearly enough. Though far too much for my liking."

His mother nodded thoughtfully before a smile began to grow on her face, and Miles could tell she was allowing a slight bit of hope to creep in.

"Oh, Miles," she said wistfully. "What if this does all work out? Oh, you could be a father. How wonderful would that be?"

Miles frowned, for the truth was, he wasn't entirely sure. His own father wasn't exactly a paragon of virtue. What sort of father would he be to a child? And what if… what if that child was afflicted as he was?

For Miles had quite a difficult time hearing nearly anything around him. He had always been that way, from the moment he was born. From what he knew, all had thought everything was fine until he came of the age when he should have been responding, should have been cooing his first words. Instead, his mother had told him, he was difficult to parent, a bit of a terror for he didn't listen to anything said to him. When he remained mute, his father had been horrified, had wanted him hidden away, pronounced dead before anyone realized that the Marquess of Dorrington had sired an idiot child.

He had blamed his wife, of course. Had said that she had

madness running through her family, and after Miles' brother, Benjamin, was born — thankfully unsoiled — the marquess had refused to attempt any further children for fear of what the result might be.

Not that his mother had any reservations about that. Miles' father spent most of his time out at his clubs, and it was no secret that he was a leech without any qualms. He gambled much of his wealth away and had no respect for Miles' mother. While he wasn't the only nobleman to be unfaithful, of course, he took no care to keep his actions discreet.

As a result, Miles and his mother had a rather close bond — for his mother was the one who had kept him out of the madhouse.

"Enough of those thoughts," she said now, a crease forming between her brows as she read his mind. "You will be a fine father. You are nothing like him."

"One never knows," Miles said with a shrug, focusing on the cup in front of him, finished with this conversation — until he finally heard a sharp rapping, and looked up to see that his mother was catching his attention by knocking on the table beside her.

"You will, Miles," she said pointedly. "And furthermore, despite Lady Fredericka's sharp eyes, it will likely take time before she realizes anything is off. You read lips better than most people listen to others. You can hear well enough so long as there is no noise behind you and the person is speaking loudly and clearly enough. You will be just fine." She paused. "Besides, she is a lovely woman. I do not think you have anything to fear."

Except that she might not want to risk having a child of her own who would be born like him. Who would have to avoid clubs, where others might think him afflicted, for he could hear nothing with the many conversations around him. Who could hardly speak at balls and the theatre, for he had difficulty making sense of the words around him. Who was threatened to be sent to the madhouse nearly every day of his life.

"We shall see," was all he said, not wishing to further worry his mother.

If it wasn't for her, he would likely still have trouble speaking. But with her persistence and the help of a specialized tutor, he had learned to speak, slowly and painstakingly. He had learned to focus and hear as best he could, to understood what he needed to do to make up for it.

He was able to pass himself off as though nothing was wrong, which was the only reason his father had ever allowed him a true existence.

And Miles was forever grateful.

He noted his mother turn to the doorway, and he followed her gaze to find that his brother had entered.

"Good morning, Miles," he said with a large smile on his affable face. He looked much like Miles, though his coloring was much darker. Miles returned his greeting, pleased to see his brother. It wasn't Benjamin's fault that he was the one favored by their father. It made sense. He was everything Miles wasn't — friendly, likable, unafflicted. "Leaving already?"

"I am," he said with a nod. "I have business to attend to today — whether I like it or not."

"Oh?"

"He's courting Lady Fredericka Ashworth!" his mother exclaimed, and Benjamin's eyebrows rose in surprise.

"Truly? I didn't know you had it in you, old chap."

Miles rolled his eyes.

"Don't tell me you have no faith in me either, brother."

"It's not that at all," Benjamin said, apparently accustomed to Miles' self-doubt. "You just haven't shown much interest in the ladies, is all. I was beginning to think that you were maybe..."

He stopped with a glance over at his mother.

"Well, at any rate, good for you, Miles, whoever you are pursuing. Good day, then! I'm off! Have some courting of my own to do."

He winked at Miles, bent over his mother's hand to place a kiss upon the back of it, and then strode jauntily out the door.

"Well, Mother, it has been a pleasure, as always," Miles said, rising as he shook his head at his brother. "I am off to visit Lady Fredericka Ashworth. Lord only knows what she has in mind, now." A thought struck him — one that would make this visit much easier. "Care to join me?"

FREDDIE PACED the drawing room of her family's London home. What had she been thinking? After her conversation with Jemima and perhaps too many cups of the ratafia spiked with Jemima's hidden brandy, she had thought her scheme splendid. She would wed a man like Miles Luxington, who would most likely leave her be.

When they were children, their families had been friends, but he had never spent a great deal of time with her and her sisters, not as his brother had. Instead, Miles would usually take out a book and hide away in one alcove or another, ignoring the lot of them. She had always thought that he didn't care for any of them, but perhaps she was wrong. Perhaps he was just shy.

At least she hoped that was the case. She had seen the wariness in his eyes at her scheme, and she had a feeling that he wasn't particularly pleased.

Perhaps he wasn't interested in her. Or interested in

marriage. For he would have been married by now, wouldn't he? She couldn't recall if she had ever heard of him being tied to a woman. She didn't think so; but then, she hadn't been paying particularly close attention. In fact, she had barely thought anything of him until her mother had dragged him across the St. Vincent ballroom just moments after she had been telling Jemima about her wish to only marry someone who would allow her to live as she wanted to and do what she chose to do. His brother Benjamin was much more charming, but Freddie doubted he was the type who would allow his wife leave to do as she pleased. Or if he did, it would only be because he was out with many other ladies. She would hope for some faithfulness.

"Fredericka?" Her mother was the only person who knew her well who called her by her full name. She always told Freddie that it was a beautiful name and that *someone* should use it. "Are you expecting a guest?"

"I'm not exactly sure," Freddie said truthfully as her mother entered the drawing room, crossing her arms over her chest and looking beyond Freddie out the front window.

"There is a carriage approaching," she said, skirting around the table in the middle of the room to look out front. "It's quite polished. A handsome pair of horses. Someone of means. Oh!"

Freddie sighed. This would have been easier without her mother present.

"It's Miles — that is, Lord Gilmore."

Apparently, her mother also thought of Miles as the bookish boy he had been and not so much the current viscount.

Freddie had always kept her distance from Miles' father, the marquess. He was a cold man, to be sure, but it was more than that — the hard glint in his eye and the way Miles flinched whenever he was near told her that there was more behind that cold exterior, more that she had no wish to uncover. Her father had always been friends with him, but never particularly close — it was their mothers who knew one another well.

And... if she wasn't mistaken, that was Miles' mother accompanying him out of the carriage.

She was surprised at the disappointment that struck her. She hadn't thought that she had been looking forward to this — whatever *this* was, with him. It would be quite a different visit with their mothers present.

"Oh, lovely!" Freddie's mother said. "Delilah is here as well."

She turned, standing next to Freddie as they awaited their guests. She might have wondered whether Miles was going to even venture out of the carriage, for he entered quite long after his mother.

"Beatrice!"

"Dee!"

Their mothers took one another by the hands in a friendly embrace of sorts before Lady Dorrington greeted Freddie, who smiled politely before Miles finally arrived in the doorway, nodding to her and her mother in greeting.

"Please, come in and sit," Freddie's mother said, leading them all over to the grouping of chairs around the table before she called for tea. Freddie sat down, spreading her hands over her knees, gripping them as they sat. This was all extremely awkward. Why had she even suggested this visit to Miles? Why had he decided to come? Why had he brought his mother?

At the very least, their mothers filled the silence while Freddie avoided his gaze uncomfortably.

"Fredericka?" her mother said, and Freddie nearly jumped in surprise, so focused she had been on *not* looking at Miles.

"Yes?"

"It must be awfully boring for the two of you to sit here while Delilah and I catch up. You and Miles should go for a walk or a drive. It is a lovely day."

"Oh, I'm not sure—" Freddie was surprised that Lady Dorrington began answering for Miles, but he interrupted her with a wave of his hand.

"It's fine, Mother," he said in his slow and steady manner. "We will see you shortly."

He stood, holding his arm out to Freddie in a rather uncomfortable manner. "Shall we?"

"Take Louisa!" Freddie's mother said with a smile before practically shooing them out the door.

They were alone. Now Freddie had to decide whether she was glad of it or not.

CHAPTER 3

*F*reddie took Miles' arm as they walked from the room before she summoned her maid to join them. She clumsily released it as she donned her bonnet, but then returned her hand as their feet hit the cobblestones of Mayfair Street. Goodness, courting was an awkward dance.

They nodded at passersby as they made their way down the street.

"Are we going to Hyde Park?" Freddie asked, breaking the silence, but Miles ignored her.

"Miles?" she squeezed his arm to capture his attention, and he turned to her with eyebrows raised.

"I'm sorry, did you say something?" he asked, and Freddie inwardly sighed. He clearly had no serious interest in her. He had likely arrived today only to be polite. His mother had probably dragged him to Freddie's house.

"I just asked if we were going to Hyde Park," she repeated herself, and he tilted his head.

"Yes, but let's stay near the pond."

"Away from everyone?" she said, narrowing her eyes, and he shrugged.

"I suppose so."

So he didn't want anyone to see the two of them together. Very well.

An awkward silence stretched between them as they continued down the street until they finally turned the corner to the park. The grass was still rather a wintery brown, despite the fact that spring was beginning to show its face as the air was becoming slightly warmer each day rather than colder.

"How are your sisters?" Miles finally asked, and Freddie smiled as she thought of them.

"They are well," she said. "Marion has two children now, while Eleanor married last year. We just found out she is expecting."

"I'm glad to hear it," he said, and Freddie was slightly perturbed by the intensity of his green stare once more.

"And your brother?" she asked.

"Benjamin is Benjamin," he said, his smile one of affection. "He loves everyone, and everyone loves him."

Freddie sensed there was more behind his words that he wasn't actually saying. It did not seem that he resented his brother, but perhaps he knew that everything others loved about his brother could not be said about him.

"I hope you did not feel undue pressure when I asked if you would call upon me," Freddie said, clenching her fingernails into her palms at her words. It had to be said, however, for it seemed to be causing the tension in the air between them.

"I was surprised more than anything," Miles said, and Freddie parted her lips in curiosity at his statement.

"Why would that be?"

"It seemed to me that you would already be spoken for," he said with a shrug, and Freddie wondered whether or not his words were meant to be a compliment.

"I am not," she said softly, not adding that she had been at one point in time — but all that had accomplished was proving that one had to be practical when it came to marriage. Following her heart had only led to betrayal.

"Listen, Freddie," he began, and she took a deep breath, ready for him to politely reject any idea of the two of them courting beyond this one walk.

"Miles, it's fine, I—"

She had been about to tell him that he didn't have to worry. That it had just been an idea that had come upon her — an impulsive idea, which was quite unlike her. That he should take her home and pretend that she had never said anything.

But then, with his eyes upon her so intently that she hadn't been able to look away, she hadn't been paying attention to where she was going. She hit a patch of slick mud, and her feet flew out from under her.

Strong arms came around just before she hit the ground, and Freddie's breath came quickly, though whether it was from the panic of nearly hitting the ground or how close Miles' face was from hers, she wasn't entirely sure.

"Are you all right?" Miles finally said before lifting her and setting her back on her feet. Freddie nodded mutely, attempting to catch hold of her emotions once more. Her reasoning had vanished for a moment as she had enjoyed Miles' touch upon her far more than she would have thought.

"Th-thank you, Miles," she finally managed, and he nodded before stepping away from her, but he did hold out his arm.

"Be sure to hold on tighter now," was all he said as he steered her closer to the lake. He drew her to the edge, the bridge just in the distance as he parted tall grass to show her the view beyond.

"The swans," she said with a smile as a couple of the majestic creatures began to swim toward them.

"It's one of my favorite views," he said, his gaze ahead of them, following the swans as they continued on their lazy circle back the way they came. "You can see the mass of people in the distance — close enough that the colors swirl together in a rainbow of color and yet far enough that they don't provide a distraction."

"A distraction?" Freddie repeated, confused. "From what?"

But Miles ignored her, continuing their walk instead, leading her down around the lake path.

"Careful," he said, pointing out another slippery patch, and she nodded as they continued. They were nearly around when Freddie saw a couple ahead of them on the path, and she stopped so quickly she nearly went off balance again.

Miles turned around, consternation on his face. "What is it?"

"Ah, nothing. Could we, ah, perhaps return the way we came?" Perspiration broke out on her brow at the thought of the approaching lord seeing her. It had been quite some time since she last saw the man who had broken her heart — and taken far more than that — and she had no wish to see him again. Particularly so happy with his new bride.

"I didn't realize you were so eager to return."

"It isn't that. It's just, I—"

But it was too late. They had seen her.

"Lady Fredericka," Lord Lovelace – Henry to her at one time but certainly no longer – said as he approached. "You look well."

A chill raced down Freddie's spine as she hugged her arms into her stomach to keep from shaking. He was ever the gentleman, as though nothing had ever occurred between them. Meanwhile, turmoil filled her stomach but she proudly managed a polite smile to match his. "Thank you. As do you, Lord Lovelace, Lady Lovelace," she said.

Lady Lovelace — a name she had scrawled upon her stationery far too often, thinking it would become her own moniker. But that had been years ago. Now she was much wiser. She knew that a good-looking man with charm could be hiding something much darker.

"Do you know Lord Gilmore?"

Lord Lovelace nodded at him. "Good to see you again, Gilmore," he said. "It has been some time."

"So it has," Miles said, looking back and forth between Freddie and Lord Lovelace with interest, as though he sensed there was more between them than a simple acquaintance.

"You shall have to call upon me some time, Lady Freder-icka," Lady Lovelace said with a genuine smile, and despite her polite answering expression, Freddie cringed inside. Call upon *Lady* Lovelace? Clearly the woman had no idea of her husband's past actions nor his duplicity.

Freddie murmured a simple "Of course," but refused to meet Lord Lovelace's gaze.

They allowed the couple to pass, and it was a few moments before Miles murmured, "Still wanting to turn around?"

Freddie glanced at him out of the corner of her eye. "Whatever you'd like," she said softly, and he nodded, his expression grim.

"Very well," he said. "Let's do one more turn and then continue to walk home."

"That sounds good," she said. "Thank you, Miles." For not asking questions. For seeming to understand that she didn't wish to speak of it any further.

But he said nothing in response, only continuing to look ahead of him.

Freddie had forgotten how little Miles spoke. When they

were children, they had chosen to basically ignore him — she and her sisters would play with Benjamin, who was much more lively. Miles was a serious sort, though he had always been kind.

"Do you have any other plans for today?" she asked, but he ignored her, instead walking determinately home. It was clear he really had no wish to continue to spend time with her. He had obviously been about to tell her so when she had slipped near the creek, but then she had completely forgotten to further pursue their conversation when her mind had been addled by his nearness and she had then been distracted by Lord Lovelace and his wife.

"You didn't have to come today if you weren't interested, Miles," she said, her gaze on the ground as she didn't entirely want to see his expression at her words — it would likely be one of relief when she released him from this day. She realized belatedly that she had squeezed his arm as she spoke.

"What was that?" he finally asked.

"I said that you didn't have to come today," she said, finally looking at him. "It was simply a suggestion. I know you are too polite to have refused, but I'd like you to know that you and I... well, we don't have to be anything beyond today's visit. I'm sorry. I shouldn't have said anything to you last night. I simply thought that since you hadn't married, and since I hadn't married, but we were both expected to, that it could be the ideal arrangement. I mean, we like each other well enough, and it would be better to be married to someone you consider a friend. But I was being foolish. You see, I had a sip too many of Jemima's hidden brandy and—"

Freddie drew a breath to calm herself. She knew she was speaking far too quickly now, but she was trying to explain herself in a way that made sense. She didn't want to look the fool, but the more he stared at her with such an intent expression, the more she felt the need to talk herself out of this. "I am pleased our mothers have had the opportunity to spend time together, but this doesn't have to go any further. We will return home, we will tell them we had a lovely walk, and then you can go home and we never have to speak again aside from the casual hello when we run into one another. Then—"

"Freddie," he said, stopping her flow of words. She had a tendency to ramble on when she was nervous, something she knew she needed to put a stop to.

"Yes?"

"We should."

"We should... what?" she asked, confused.

"We should do it."

"I'm sorry, Miles, I don't—"

"Freddie... would you marry me?"

CHAPTER 4

*M*iles didn't know who was more shocked at his question — Freddie... or he.

She stopped walking, her feet rooted to the ground as she stared at him with her mouth wide open.

"Pardon me?"

"I asked if you would marry me," he repeated, wondering if she truly hadn't heard him. After all, he asked people to repeat themselves quite often.

"Why?" she asked, and when he saw a bench, he led her off of the path toward it, sitting down next to her so that their knees were nearly touching. The view in front of him was one he longed to return to in order to paint, but now was not the time to think of such a thing.

"It's as you said," he explained, trying to make sense of it himself. The words had spewed forth, in part to get her to stop talking, stop questioning herself. There was clearly some past history with Lord Lovelace, which had only seemed to put further doubts in herself. Why he thought proposing marriage was a solution to increasing her self-worth he had no idea, but the more he thought on it, the more he was warming to the idea. "We get on well enough with one another. Our mothers are great friends. It's a sound idea."

As she had spoken, her words began to make sense and he had been stolen by the thought – why not? Then he could have this all done, without the need to endure the courting business.

If he married her, he would also no longer have to put himself through the agony of pursuing any other. She was pleasant enough and she would do as she wished without requiring constant attention from him. His father would approve of her, and his marriage would perhaps be enough to keep the marquess from following through on the threats he continually uttered.

But... he was never one to make a rash decision. Perhaps he should have thought this through.

"Well, one good reason would be that perhaps you would like to wait for a woman you are passionately in love with."

Miles laughed uncomfortably. He had thought himself to be in love once, but that had been ruined with one simple admission. When she had found out about his impairment, she had been done with him. Now, he just needed someone who would fit the required role of viscountess and one day marchioness.

"I don't think that will ever happen."

"Why not?"

"It just won't," he said, more sharply than he intended. "Anyway, it would likely work well between us."

"There is one thing — something that is very important," she said, looking at him intently, and he stared at her, waiting for her request.

Of course, there would be something else. Why else would she want to marry *him*? Would she want the ability to take a lover? Maybe that was why she actually wanted to wed

— she was in love with a footman or something of the sort and needed someone to hide their affair. That, he realized with a fierce and unexpected surge of possessiveness, would never happen. If he was going to take a wife, she would be his, damn it.

Then another thought occurred to him — perhaps she was with child. Could he raise another man's child as his own?

He was so caught up in his imaginings that he nearly missed her request.

"I would like the ability to continue my work without restriction."

Confusion rippled through him, and he frowned. "Your work?"

She nodded briefly, looking down at her hands once more. He wished she wouldn't do that. It was hard to watch her lips with her head tilted downward.

"I… well, I suppose you could say I like to… tinker with things. Find better ways to make them work. My father taught me how to woodwork when I was young, and since then, there are a few apparatuses that I have devised to help around the house."

"Like what?" he asked, fascinated for a moment. The woman was beautiful, friendly, and now intelligent enough to have apparently innovated a new concept?

"Nothing much, really," she said, red staining her cheeks. "One is a device of sorts." She began to explain it, but she continued to look away and he struggled to hear her. Something to do with eggs and tea.

"Interesting," he murmured, wishing he knew more of what she said.

"It's nothing." She waved a hand in the air, perhaps mistaking his nonchalance for disinterest.

"I do not mind if you want to spend time on such work,

Freddie," he said instead, knowing it was what she wanted to hear. "You can do as you please."

"Excellent," she said, a true smile finally beaming across her face as she clapped her hands together.

Miles suddenly had the feeling that she could care less who she married as long as he provided for her while allowing her to do as she pleased. A sense of unease filled him. He was not typically an impulsive man. Now he remembered why. Some decisions, however hastily made, could not be undone.

"When... when would you like to be married?"

The first glimmer of what he guessed was hesitancy crossed her face. How much had she thought this through herself? Had she considered that this would be a pairing for life? That, while they may never be a couple in love, they would share living space, have adjoining bedrooms, possibly create children together?

He voiced none of that, though, as he stood from the bench, holding his arm out to her once more. The spring day was crisp and clear, the leaves on the trees beginning to turn green as they began to flourish around the Serpentine.

"I suppose we could wait until after Easter and long enough for the banns to be read," he said. "Would that work for you?"

"Of course. I do not have many people I would like to invite to attend the wedding. My family, of course, and some of my friends, but that would suffice. My mother would like to invite half the *ton*, I'm sure, but she was able to do so for my sisters, so it should be fine. Well," she said, her voice returning to the firm businesslike tone once more, "shall we return and share the good news with our mothers?"

Miles nodded. His mother would be thrilled. He was glad someone would be. He liked Freddie — truly, he did. But he wondered just how he would spend the rest of his life next to perfection and not feel the worse for it all.

* * *

THIS WAS GOOD, Freddie told herself as she sat on the sofa while their mothers planned excitedly.

Lady Dorrington and Freddie's mother had been shocked yet thrilled when she and Miles had surprised them with their announcement. Miles was currently speaking with her father to make everything official, but it had basically been determined.

Freddie sat there as the women spoke to one another so quickly she had to rapidly blink as she attempted to take it all in. She was somewhat stunned. This was what she had wanted, yes, but now it was becoming so... real. She worried her lip as she wondered... had she done the right thing? She had acted impulsively, which was not like her. She usually took more time to ponder something over, to plan and decide all of the steps. This had *seemed* a good plan, a safe plan, but now she was realizing just how permanent it was. And was it fair to Miles?

But he had suggested it — so perhaps he wanted a marriage of convenience as much as she did? She sighed, leaning her elbows on her knees and placing her head in her hands.

He was a good man. She might never fall passionately in love with him, but she had done that once already, and look what had come of it — her, nearly ruined, while the man she had thought she would spend the rest of her life loving was now waking up with someone else.

No, love was not important. It was about stability and finding a husband who wouldn't interfere with how she wanted to live.

This was for the best, she told herself as she sat up straight when Miles and her father returned.

"Well, then," her father said, his booming voice filling the drawing room. "My last daughter is to be married and will become Lady Gilmore. A happy day for us all."

Freddie smiled at her father, but then her gaze flicked to Miles. His face was as stoic as always, his shoulders set as though he had just agreed to a life sentence in Newgate. Freddie lifted her chin in an attempt to show her pleasure, despite the unease settling into her stomach.

She took a deep breath.

This would be fine.

It had to be.

* * *

"You're getting married?"

Jemima's shocked face spoke volumes. Celeste's jaw dropped open while Rebecca wore a slight look of relief. Freddie had a feeling that Rebecca had always felt slightly guilty for marrying Val, despite the fact that the two of them were more in love than any couple Freddie had ever seen.

"Yes," Freddie said with a quick nod, "in three weeks' time."

"Three weeks?" Celeste managed. "That is not much time at all."

"No," Freddie said, swallowing her own slight panic, "but we are old enough. Might as well. And besides, if we wait too long then everyone will be in the country for the summer. I would love for you all to be there."

"Of course we will," said Jemima, her blue eyes wide. "But, Freddie... you danced with him for the first time but *days* ago."

"I know," Freddie acknowledged. "It seems rather sudden.

But this is what I always wanted. And don't forget, I have known him my entire life. It shall be fine."

She attempted a smile to reassure her friends. The truth was, however, she was anything *but* calm about the entire situation. For the more time she had to think about it, the more anxious she became.

What would it be like to be someone's *wife*? Even if they remained primarily friends, they would be managing a household together, would share a bed some nights, perhaps have children together one day. She nearly lost her breath at the thought. Instead of being filled solely with worry, however, she also found herself overtaken with nervous excitement. Which was strange. Had she been asked before, she wasn't sure if she would have said she had any attraction to Miles. He was good looking, to be sure, but his stoicism gave him such a serious countenance that she had never actually considered him much at all.

Now that she thought of being with him, however, a tingle coursed through her — one that started at her toes and raced up her body. What would it be like, she wondered, to be with one another? To kiss him? To—

"Freddie?"

Her attention returned to the room with a jolt.

"Yes?" she said quickly.

"Will you need any help finding a dress? Choosing flowers? Planning the wedding breakfast?"

Celeste was becoming excited at the prospect now, while Jemima looked a little green at the topic. Rebecca simply smiled demurely.

Freddie chuckled.

"Thank you, but I think my mother has it all well in hand. Though I may solicit some help in choosing a dress. As much as I love the beauty of lace and adornments, if it were up to my mother I would be covered in so much fabric and ornamentation I would resemble a decorated banquet table."

"That we can do," Rebecca said, and Freddie smiled her thanks.

"Did you speak to him about your work?" Jemima asked, and Freddie nodded.

"He did not protest at all, though he seemed a bit apprehensive," she said with a shrug.

"How soon did you bring it up?" Jemima asked shrewdly. "Maybe he realized that was why you were marrying him."

That hadn't really occurred to Freddie, though it should have. Miles was no fool. She hadn't been overly complimentary of him besides telling him that she was looking for someone who would appreciate her for who she was, provide for her, and be friends with her. He had still asked her to marry him, so she had assumed that he was looking for the same sort of partnership. Perhaps she needed to put more thought into her words and interactions with him.

"You're right," she said. "I shall make sure he knows that there will be more to our marriage than completely separate lives. That I look forward to being with my friend if nothing else."

"That might help," Rebecca said, though she looked dubious. But Freddie couldn't help that she would never have a marriage like Rebecca's — one that was centered around the love the two of them shared more than anything else.

"There's nothing to worry about," Freddie said, hoping she sounded surer than she felt. "All will be fine. I know what I'm doing."

If only that were the truth.

CHAPTER 5

*H*ad anyone ever devised a carriage with a trap door in it so that when one needed to escape, there was an easy way out? Freddie hoped not. For she wondered if Miles would currently be considering using such an option.

She had insisted that they arrive well ahead of schedule. Freddie despised it when brides were late to their own weddings. What was the point of making everyone else wait? All it did was show disregard for the worth of their time. Her father had chuckled at her when she had called upstairs for him to hurry up, but he knew how important it was to her to arrive when scheduled.

Except once they arrived, she realized that Miles was not yet there. She couldn't see his carriage anywhere, and she urged her parents to disembark first, asking her father to return with an update.

"He's not here just yet, Fred," he said upon his return, using his pet name for her. "I'm sure he's running behind just slightly. He'll be here any moment."

He hefted his rather rotund body into the seat across

from her, his smile more forced than Freddie would have liked.

"You're just saying that to appease me," she said, narrowing her eyes at him, and his cheeks slightly reddened even as he shook his head vigorously. Too vigorously.

"Of course not!" he insisted, but Freddie knew her father far better than that. He was a good man, one who had sired three daughters and had never once made any of them feel as though he would have preferred a son — despite the fact that it meant his title would go to their cousin Peter. So be it, her father had always said, for Peter was a good enough man and already had two sons of his own.

Freddie sighed, tilting her head back to rest it on the squab behind her, but remembering at the last moment that if she did so, she would destroy the intricate chignon her maid had fashioned.

"What if he doesn't come?" she asked nervously, tapping her foot on the floor of the carriage. "I would be a laughingstock."

The truth was, she had been fearful of this far before they had arrived at the church. Since the day of their walk and betrothal, Miles had not called at all, though his mother had visited quite often to help decide on wedding details. She told Freddie that Miles was seeing to matters out in the country before their wedding day and that he could hardly wait until they were wed.

Freddie wasn't so sure, as it seemed that her former fears were coming true.

In a way, maybe this was for the best. For there were things about her that she hadn't told him — things that a future husband should likely know. Only, had she shared her secret, he would have turned her away. It made her feel a fraud to have deceived him, but perhaps he would never need to know.

"Do not be silly," her father said now. "Of course Miles is coming. He is too good a man to stand you up. And he is lucky to have you, Fred, don't forget that."

Freddie nodded. No man would ever be as wonderful as her father, that was for certain. And if he thought that Miles would be true to his word, then she should believe him.

She took a deep breath.

"But what if he doesn't?"

Her father finally just sighed and shrugged.

"Then he doesn't."

* * *

MILES HAD SPENT FAR TOO LONG that morning pacing his bedchamber, trying to decide if he should go through with this wedding. Could he be the husband Freddie deserved? She had always been such a cheerful, fun-loving girl who had grown into a spirited woman. He knew he could be down-right miserable. He also wasn't about to be spending days and nights as part of the social scene, attending balls and operas, theatres and parties. Would she expect that? What would she do when he had no interest in accompanying her?

He had no wish to leave her the day of the wedding, but would that not be far more bearable than a lifetime of regret?

Finally, he had caught sight of himself in the mirror and had reminded himself that Freddie had wanted this. While he had ultimately requested her hand, this had been her idea from the start. He would have been content with just one dance.

And, he realized now as his carriage pulled up to the church, part of him, a part buried deep within him, was excited about marriage to Freddie. She had always been beautiful, but when she bestowed that wide, winning smile on *him* it was as though the entire world became brighter.

She would bring vibrancy into his life that had been lacking from it for far too long. He only hoped that he wouldn't squander it.

Then there was the fact that she would be his. That he could walk through that connecting door whenever he chose and lie with his *wife*. His pulse began to pound in his ears at even the thought of it, and he had to push the image far from his mind — for the time being, at least.

He pulled out his pocket watch as St. George's appeared through the window of the carriage and realized that he was more than a quarter of an hour late, which was not particularly acceptable for a bridegroom.

Well, regardless of his tardiness, he was here. He had decided to arrive alone. His brother would stand up for him but would be arriving with his parents, and Miles couldn't entertain the thought of being trapped in a carriage, even for a short ride, with his father.

The church and all it held seemed to heave a collective sigh of relief when Miles walked through the door, and a pang of guilt lanced through him. If the guests had been wondering whether or not he would be arriving, what must Freddie have been thinking? He could be the first to admit that he hadn't been particularly attentive to her since they had announced their betrothal. The truth, however, was that he hadn't wanted to risk her learning his secret. If she was his wife, she would be compelled to keep it to herself. But she could easily break off their engagement if she knew him to be near completely deaf. Just as Rosemary had.

The fact he had kept it from her made him the worst sort of boor.

The colored sunlight streamed in through the high windows as he took his place at the front of the church after greeting a few distant relatives and some friends. Miles kept his circle of acquaintants small, and it seemed

Freddie did the same as her side was equally as empty as his.

Thank goodness. Miles couldn't remember ever having so many people staring at him before, all at one time. He hated it.

Miles glanced over at his mother, seeing that her eyes were shining, glistening with unshed tears. Oh, dear. He could only imagine what she would be like once the ceremony began. His father fastened a hardened gaze upon him before standing and approaching him. Miles stiffened, willing his father to sit back down, to leave him be, today of all days.

"So you've found yourself a bride." His father's lips twisted into a grin. Miles couldn't hear him — his father spoke softly on purpose, but he could read what he was saying. "Didn't think you had it in you."

Miles said nothing, not wanting to provide his father any satisfaction to know that any of his words registered.

"Do not ruin this for yourself," his father said, pointing a finger at him before returning to his seat as anger began to simmer in Miles' belly. He refused to allow any emotion to show on his face, to provide any other with the knowledge of how he was reacting to his father's words.

Instead, he looked around the church once more.

He nodded in greeting at the two women standing up for Freddie as bridesmaids — her sisters. He hadn't seen them in some time, but they looked just like her, though one was a bit taller and the other a bit wider. Both were beaming as brightly as their mother.

He wondered how long Freddie would make him wait here at the front of the church. He supposed he deserved to stand here alone for quite some time, as he had seen her carriage waiting out front. How long had she been sitting there? Weren't brides supposed to keep everyone waiting?

But then his thoughts were interrupted when the organ began to play. He felt the vibrations first through the floor, but the organ was loud enough that strains of the music reached him. The chords were long and melancholic, and he wondered why a wedding song wouldn't be more upbeat and happier. Perhaps it was a sign of what was to come, he thought nervously as his stomach tightened.

Suddenly there was some movement at the back of the church, and the congregation stood as one. He couldn't hear as to whether there were any sighs or murmured words regarding the bride, but he could tell by the expressions of those he could see that Freddie must look a wonder. Women were smiling in appreciation, while many of the men — too many men, he decided — looked far too admiring. This woman was going to be his wife, damn it, and they would best look away for—

Then Freddie stepped into his line of vision.

Miles' breath caught, and he forgot all of his reservations. No longer did he care that he would be the object of attention in front of so many. No longer did he worry about what kind of husband he would make. No longer was he concerned that Freddie might find out all that was wrong with him.

To say she looked beautiful was an understatement. She could not have been more stunning unless the sun itself was directly behind her as she walked down the aisle.

She was dressed in powder blue, with an intricate lace overlay atop the bodice. Cap sleeves showed her slender arms, while the gown descended in waves to the floor. A matching blue ribbon was tied around her tiny waist, while she clutched in her hands a bouquet of white flowers — what kind they were, Miles had no idea, for he knew nothing of flowers. Her hand was placed upon the arm of her father, who was currently looking at Miles as though imploring him to take good care of his daughter, his youngest, his baby girl.

Miles nodded at him, but he could not take his eyes off of Freddie. Her brown eyes looked wider than they ever had, her dark colored hair pulled back away from her face and covered with a headpiece of beautiful jewels and flowers matching those she carried in her bouquet. Two small ringlets dancing around her cheeks which were filled with the slightest hint of pink, matching those bow lips, currently curled into a hesitant smile.

Miles did the best he could to return her smile, to help her to feel comfortable in this decision they were making together — one which they both seemed to be questioning, yet continuing on with anyway.

A slight tear fell from Freddie's eye as she kissed her father's cheek, but she brushed it away as he whispered something in her ear that made her laugh.

Then, finally, she was left alone with Miles, the two of them, together, standing in front of the vicar.

Miles took a deep breath, narrowed his eyes, and focused on every word the vicar said. This would hardly be the time to make a fool of himself.

"Dearly beloved, we are gathered together here in the sight of God, and in the face of this congregation, to join together this Man and this Woman in holy Matrimony…" he began and Miles listened intently, awaiting his cue as the vicar continued to drone on.

He answered, "I will," when appropriate, as Freddie did the same — thankfully, without hesitation.

He had spent some time consulting the Book of Common Prayer, attempting to memorize the words he must say to Freddie. But when he'd first seen her, all thought had fled, and even now he was having difficulty remembering the words.

Miles looked to the vicar to see what he was saying, as he could only catch some of his words, so echoey was the Church of Saint George around them.

"I, Miles, take thee, Fredericka, to my wedded wife, to have and to hold from this day forward, for better for worse, for richer, for poorer, in sickness and in health, to love and to cherish, till death us do part, according to God's holy ordinance; and thereto I plight thee my troth," he repeated, not realizing until he was finished that he had said all of the words staring at the vicar, who was now looking at him with some consternation. He turned his gaze back to Freddie with some trepidation.

And was not surprised to find a vexed gaze staring back at him.

CHAPTER 6

*W*as the man interested in marrying her or the vicar?

Freddie fumed inwardly. Did Miles care so little, or did he so despise the thought of marrying her, that he couldn't even look at her?

She had to admit that while Miles had always been a pleasant-looking man, today there was something additionally attractive about him. She could have said that it was, perhaps, his attire. But there was nothing particularly unusual about his white linen shirt, black jacket, and black breeches. He was adorned in his usual evening wear, the only difference being that it was currently morning.

No, what it had been was the way he had looked at her. His eyes had practically burned into her as she walked down the aisle, and for a moment, she had wondered if, perhaps, he really and truly did want her, more so than this being the result of a practical agreement they had made with each other.

Then the ceremony had started, and she didn't think he had looked at her even once since.

When it was her turn to say the words, she spoke them slowly, carefully, staring at Miles the entire time so that he would see the proper way for people to pledge themselves to one another for the rest of their lives.

Freddie was somewhat mollified by the fact that he seemed to have realized the error of his ways. For when it was time to place the ring on her finger, he did, at least, properly regard her, though he spent an equal amount of time staring at the vicar.

His warmth flooded through her white satin glove as he took her hand, and her skin tingled at the glint in his green eyes when he spoke to her.

"With this ring I thee wed, with my body I thee worship, and with all my worldly goods I thee endow. In the Name of the Father, and of the Son, and of the Holy Ghost. Amen."

When the vicar joined their hands together, saying, "Those whom God hath joined together let no man put asunder," Freddie's heart really and truly began to beat hard.

She had been nervous before, had wondered if she had made the right decision. But somehow she hadn't quite realized just how... *absolute* this all was.

She and Miles were married and would spend the rest of their lives together. She swallowed hard.

There was no going back now.

* * *

"Congratulations!"

"Welcome to the family!"

"Well done!"

Miles had never spoken to so many different people at one time in his life. Sure, he had been in attendance at social events, but he had been able to remain in the background. There was none of that to be had today. No, today he and

41

Freddie were the focus of all, and he sorely wished this damned wedding breakfast would finish and he could leave to find solace in his own home. It was far too difficult to pay attention to all of them, and he was unable to keep them all on one side of him so he knew he had missed more than one comment.

If it had been up to him, they would not even have had a wedding breakfast, but Freddie's family had insisted and he didn't think it prudent to refuse. She wasn't getting much of a husband — the least he could do was allow her to have the wedding she wanted.

Between her sisters, her mother, and her friends, he hadn't actually seen much of Freddie since the wedding had ended. They'd had a carriage ride alone together between the church and her parents' Mayfair home, but it lasted only minutes and they had spent most of it staring out the window. He could tell Freddie was upset with him, and he had figured out why, but he wasn't going to apologize for not looking at her during the ceremony — that was ridiculous. And he certainly wasn't going to explain just why he hadn't been.

Now he found himself lost in the crowd of people within the Ashworth drawing room. There were so many conversations ebbing and flowing around him, words spoken to him that he couldn't hear through the cacophony of noise around them that the sensation of being overwhelmed was beginning. He stole a glance over at Freddie. She looked positively radiant with all of the attention and the well-wishing. She could have it. He had no time for it.

A hand clasped his shoulder, and he turned to find himself facing the Duke of Wyndham. Miles didn't know him well, but he was aware that all the talk had been that the man had been supposed to marry Freddie, so Miles hadn't been particularly pleased to find him at the wedding. But, apparently, the duke had married a friend of hers instead so he supposed he had nothing to worry about, so long as Freddie didn't hold a secret tendre for him. He had never asked.

"You look as though you could use a drink," the duke said, and Miles nodded.

"I suppose I could."

The two of them left the drawing room containing mostly women, taking refuge in the library. Miles indicated two of the winged armchairs in the center of the room, refusing the duke's flask as he walked over to the sideboard where Rothwell kept his spirits.

"Save that," Miles said dryly. "You never know when you might need it."

"Truer words were never spoken," the duke said, and Miles recalled that the man had not been born into the nobility but had surprisingly inherited his title. It had been the talk of the *ton*, though it wasn't until recently that the duke and his family had spent much time in the public eye. Miles held up a bottle of whiskey as he looked over his shoulder at the duke, who shook his head. "I'm a brandy man, if Rothwell has it," the duke said, and Miles nodded when he located it.

When he turned from the sideboard, he saw the duke looking at him expectantly, and Miles realized that he must have missed something.

"I'm sorry, what was that?" he asked, feigning nonchalance.

"I asked how it felt to be a married man," the duke repeated as he accepted the proffered glass.

Miles shrugged. "I cannot say I feel altogether different than I did a few hours ago, except for being slightly less nervous."

The duke laughed, though his countenance held little humor.

"I wouldn't like to go through the ceremony twice," he said, though his smile was not strained but rather fond.

"You and your wife…" Miles began, unsure of how to ask what he wished as he took a seat across the table.

"We are a love match," the duke said, taking pity on him, and Miles nodded, leaning back in his chair as he took a long swallow of the brandy. "Lady Fredericka — that is, Lady Gilmore now — she seems to be a good woman. Though you likely already know that."

"I do," Miles agreed. "We have known one another since we were children, though I am a slight bit older than her." *And not nearly as friendly*, he added in his mind.

"If you're wondering what occurred between us, the answer is absolutely nothing," the duke said, perhaps sensing Miles' hesitation in speaking with him. "Our mothers envisioned a match, but Lady Fredericka and I soon learned that we did not suit. And then there was Rebecca."

Miles wondered for a moment if the now-Duchess of Wyndham had not already been part of the duke's life whether Freddie would have married him or not. Then he decided he didn't want to think on it any longer, for he had a feeling he knew what the answer would be, and he actually somewhat liked Wyndham.

"It doesn't matter," Miles replied, attempting nonchalance, although Wyndham slightly snorted as he looked at him.

"It will. I would pummel any man I thought might garner an ounce of Rebecca's affections. Lady Fredericka will make a suitable wife, Gilmore."

"I am aware," he said tersely. He had known Freddie far longer than Wyndham had — who was the man to suddenly act her protector?

"I don't mean anything by it," Wyndham said — or at least Miles thought that was what he said — as he spoke so softly Miles couldn't make him out and the duke was looking off to the side.

"All is well, Wyndham," Miles said, not wishing to speak of it any longer. "Thank you for the suggestion of a drink."

"Anytime," Wyndham said with a grin as they rose, but then he paused for a moment, his brow furrowed as though he wasn't certain if he should say anything further. "Say, Gilmore, your father… I've heard a bit of talk about him."

"Oh?" Miles said, crossing his arms over his chest. This couldn't be good.

Wyndham ran a hand through his blond hair. "Is it… true what is said about him?"

"What have you heard?" Miles asked through tight lips.

"Just that he's a bit of a brute," Wyndham said with a shrug. "Enjoys the ladies offered at the clubs and all sorts, but isn't always exactly… gentle with them."

Miles stared at the duke, caught between admitting the truth of the man who sired him but little else, and covering for the sake of his family. It was not a question that a man raised in the *ton* would have asked. But it was one of a man who cared for the well-being of a lady.

Finally, the duke's open, honest expression was the deciding factor.

"You're right about it all," Miles said stiffly. "But not to worry. I will keep Freddie far, far away from him. She'll be safe with me, Wyndham."

Relief overtook the Duke's face. "Glad to hear it," he said. "For I was beginning to be somewhat worried—" He stopped abruptly when Miles took a step toward him. "Yes?"

"I believe it is my job to ensure Freddie's protection now," Miles said but softened slightly when he saw the concern on the other man's face. Miles knew Wyndham was just doing what he thought was right, though it irked him to think of another man looking after his wife.

"Thank you for your concern," Miles managed, swallowing his pride and taking the man's hand in a firm handshake. "And thank you for coming this morning."

"Hopefully we will be seeing more of one another," the duke said. "I could use some friends."

Miles felt the same, but he didn't know how to put it in words without sounding ridiculous, so he just nodded and opened the door to return to the party, however reluctant he was to do so.

And found his father on the other side.

CHAPTER 7

*F*reddie took her seat at the place of honor in the middle of the breakfast table, greeting the family and friends that had joined them.

Her cheeks were becoming quite cramped from the smile she had forced upon her face for the past few hours. She had convinced herself she had made the right decision. Miles Luxington was a good man, she inwardly repeated. One who had no qualms about her being the woman she was meant to be. He wouldn't care that she didn't fit the mold of wife most were looking for, would he?

Only he hadn't said a word to her all morning — unless one counted the vows that he had recited back to the vicar. He hadn't even been able to look at her during the ceremony. Had he really been that reluctant to marry her?

She had been annoyed, true, but even more so she had doubted herself. What was it about her that bothered him? Could he not even spare a moment to tell her how she looked, even if the compliment was contrived?

Freddie knew that it was rather vain to be thinking thus and even more so to be upset about such a thing, but she couldn't help it. This was her wedding day, and whether or not she and her husband actually felt anything more than friendliness for one another, he could at least spare a glance her way or a word or two of compliment.

"Where is Lord Gilmore?" her sister, Marian, asked from her place beside her, while an empty chair currently sat next to Freddie's other elbow.

"I'm sure he will be here shortly," Freddie said, taking a large sip of her wine. *He better be here shortly.* She had already waited for him long enough at the church. Surely he wouldn't make them all wait here as well.

His father, Lord Dorrington, entered the room and took his seat. He smiled at Freddie, a smile she struggled to return. There was something about him that sent unease rippling down her spine. It had always been that way, and she wasn't entirely sure why. He blustered quite a bit and she had heard rumors that he was rather uncouth. She hadn't, however, seen any of it firsthand, and Freddie wasn't one who put a great deal of stock in gossip.

The look he sent her way now, however… it was one of triumph from a man who had won something. She didn't see how she was such a tremendous catch for his son, so, unsure, she turned away as she scanned the room for Miles. Where was he?

At last she heard the tread of a step behind her, and she turned to find him pulling out his chair.

"I'm glad you have finally made your presence known," she said from the corner of her mouth once he sat, keeping her gaze forward, not wanting to show her vexation to all in attendance.

"Freddie!" her sister hissed from beside her, but she turned to her left instead to see how Miles would react. Rousing her anger even further, she saw that he had no response whatsoever. His features were set in a grim, even line, and as he sat down he didn't even look at her but simply stared at his plate in front of him. He ate mechanically, without a word to anyone.

"Is something not to your satisfaction?" she murmured in a low voice, but still he said nothing, completely ignoring her. Freddie closed her eyes and took a breath before turning to him once more.

"How is your breakfast?" she asked tersely and directly, and this time he finally did respond.

"My breakfast is fine."

"And your wine?"

"Fine."

Freddie guessed she could ask him how anything in the world was — the weather, his finances, the bloody King of England — and all he would say was, "It is fine."

But she wasn't going to give anyone anything to talk about following their wedding, besides how beautiful everything was — except for her, as, apparently, judging by her new husband, she was nothing to comment upon.

As soon as the breakfast was over, he rose, nodded to them all and excused himself, leaving the entire table staring at Freddie, who pushed the smile back onto her face and pretended all was fine, just as Miles would have said.

Everything, however, was clearly not.

His wedding day could not have been worse.

Miles cursed as he began the walk from the Ashforth residence to the townhouse he had secured for himself and Freddie.

Freddie — his new bride.

What had he been thinking? He must have been seized by a moment of insanity when he had asked her to marry him.

Perhaps his father was right. Perhaps he did belong in a home somewhere, away from the rest of society, if he had thought for a moment that marriage to her would solve his problems.

But no — he knew now it would only make everything worse.

She was far too spirited, a fact that he should have known and recognized. Lady Fredericka Ashworth had always known what she wanted and had gone after it. This time, it had been him, and he had been weak enough to succumb.

It would only be a matter of time until she discovered that he could hardly hear anything. She was far too perceptive, too observant for her own good. She was already looking at him strangely, as though she knew something was not quite right.

But it wasn't something. It was him.

She had smiled throughout the wedding ceremony, smiled through the breakfast, exuberance in her voice and a good word and time for everyone in attendance — even his father. If only she knew.

Why did she feel the need to make everyone feel welcome? It was so insincere. She was jubilant about everything. How would he know when she was actually excited about something? It was driving him mad — nearly as much as his father on the other side of the table, leering at him.

During their conversation following his drink with Wyndham, his father had told him in no uncertain terms that he was to keep his secret, especially from his bride. For if her family found out, his father was sure it would be their ruin.

He also provided him with a warning – that he had no desire for more descendants who bore the same abnormality as Miles. How Miles was supposed to prevent that, he wasn't exactly sure, but the marquess didn't seem to care that it was out of his control.

Miles kicked at a loose pebble on the street, knowing that he should currently be seated next to his wife. She seemed to be fine on her own, however, having had a much better breakfast with those around her than she would have if he had remained present. He had left the carriage for her and had provided his driver instructions to bring her to their townhouse whenever she was ready. She could spend the day with the people she truly cared about before having to join him.

He was a miserable boor. What better time for her to realize such a thing than her wedding day? Then, at the very least, she would not have any misconceptions in regard to what this marriage would truly be like.

It was for the best.

* * *

FREDDIE HAD SHOULDERED the full weight of sympathetic pity that could possibly be piled upon her from all in attendance at their wedding breakfast. She had excused Miles, saying that he had fallen ill, unfortunately, but she was well aware that most saw it for what it was — her attempt to cover the fact that he had left his own wedding breakfast.

And his wife.

This was what she wanted, she reminded herself. A marriage that fulfilled her duty and provided her with all of the comforts of life, so that she wouldn't have to rely on the charity of her sisters and their husbands as she aged.

Yet a niggling presence in the back of her mind told her that she knew better. That secretly, deep within her, she longed for something more. Something truer. That Miles had been more than a random selection.

Here she was, sitting alone now in the carriage. Most of her belongings had already been moved to the townhouse she and Miles would now share in a less prestigious yet still affluent square within Mayfair. Miles had allowed her the opportunity to design it as she wished, and she was eager to become mistress in her own home.

But what did that mean regarding her relationship with her husband?

She would soon find out.

It wasn't long before the carriage came to a stop and the driver assisted her down the steps so that she wouldn't trip on her voluminous skirts. Freddie fought down the irritation that her husband wasn't here to help her. At the very least, could he not have left the house to greet her?

She stalked boldly down the walk and up the front steps. She was about to lift the brass knocker when she realized that this was *her* house, and she opened the door at nearly the same time the butler did from within.

"Lady Gilmore, welcome home," said the wizened old man in greeting, his cheeks wrinkling into a smile. He had previously been in the employ of Miles' parents but had chosen to accompany Miles to his new residence.

"Thank you Bartleby," she said, appreciating the fact that *someone* was happy to see her. "I am pleased to have you here."

He nodded.

"Would you like me to find Mrs. Atkins to show you to your room?"

"First I think I will speak to my husband."

"Very good, my lady. You will find him in his study. Would you like me to show you the way?"

"Thank you, Bartleby, but I believe I remember it."

She had previously visited the house with her mother and sisters. She had hoped to explore it with her husband, but he apparently had already become familiar with it.

"Miles."

She called his name as she entered the study, placing her small reticule down on one of the side tables before slowly pulling each finger from its hole in her glove, then sliding it off and repeating the motions with the other one. Sighing, she set them both down next to her reticule.

Her husband didn't even look up.

Freddie was tempted to turn around and walk out the door, ignoring him as he continually did her, but she was becoming too angry for that. She strode into the room now, placing her bare hands on top of the desk he sat behind.

He sat up abruptly as though surprised to see her, the pen in his hand leaving a jagged line upon the page in front of him.

"Freddie!" he exclaimed. "You're home."

"Yes," she said, the word practically hissing out of her lips. "I am home. In *our* home."

"I see that."

Was she seeing things, or did the slightest bit of apprehension pass over his eyes?

"You *left* me at our wedding breakfast. Alone. Without a word."

At the very least, he looked somewhat chagrined at her words. "Yes, sorry about that, Freddie. I was done with the whole charade."

"Done with it?" she said, knowing her mouth was agape, but unable to close it. "The breakfast was for *you*, Miles. For *us*. And you just... left? Why? I don't understand."

"I apologized, Freddie. That should be enough. Besides, the whole thing was for you, anyhow. No one cared whether or not I was there."

At the very least, he hadn't returned his attention to the papers in front of him.

"Of course they cared," she said, lifting her hands and placing them on her hips as she walked away from him to look out the window, which faced the back of the house to the mews beyond. "I cared," she added softly.

"Look, Freddie, those types of events are just not for me. I stayed as long as I could."

Freddie turned back to him.

"Why didn't you say anything to me? I would have come with you."

His green eyes widened. "You would have?"

"Of course," she said, waving her hands in front of her. "This day was about us, Miles. We may not exactly be a love match, but this is still our marriage, the beginning of the rest of our lives."

"You seemed to be having a fine time without speaking to me at all," he said with a shrug, though he was standing now, leaning back against a cabinet beside the desk.

"I spoke to you plenty," she said, their gazes locked on one another. "You ignored me. It seems to have become a habit already."

He looked slightly uncomfortable but shrugged.

"Isn't that what you wanted? To be left alone to live your life the way you choose to? Or is that only when it's convenient for you?"

Freddie opened her mouth to retort but then closed it again. What was she supposed to say? For he was right. It was exactly what she had said to him.

When she looked at him now, however, a small bit of longing coursed through her. He had always been so standoffish that in their youth she hadn't given him much thought. He had always simply been Miles. Miles, deep in his books, Miles, who chose to do as he pleased without regard for the rest of them. Miles, who never caused any discord. Miles, who could be in a room and one wouldn't even know it.

Now she was looking at her husband and realized she wanted more than that. She wanted Miles, a man who would treat her as his wife. Her gaze ran over his smart black jacket, his fitted breeches, and the simple waistcoat. He always wore clothing that made him rather indistinguishable, and yet, as the man standing in front of her now, he cut a fine figure. One that she realized, with a slight bit of panic, she wanted to see more of.

She was no fool. She knew that with marriage would come nights together, and the *act* of being husband and wife. In fact, she knew far more of that act then she cared to — a matter that scared her, for she was unsure exactly how Miles would react when he learned the truth.

They were married now, however, so he couldn't leave her once he knew it — could he?

"I suppose I thought… I thought that we would still be a *partnership*, which a husband and wife should be together."

"Well," he said, taking a seat at his desk once more. "You thought wrong. You can't have it every way you'd like, Freddie, whenever you feel the time is right. I am not your puppet. Now, I have much to do before dinner, so perhaps you will leave me be?"

Freddie swallowed hard. Miles had more backbone than she had assumed. She thought she had wanted to marry a man who would be malleable and much easier to assert her will over. One who wouldn't care what she did or who she was.

She was getting her wish, but not in the way she had pictured it. Miles was proving himself to be far more demanding and interested in her than she would have imagined.

The part that scared her?

She liked it.

CHAPTER 8

*F*reddie pushed an errant lock of hair behind her ear as she bent over the worktable in front of her. Half of what was supposed to be a library was serving as her workshop. She missed the large outbuilding that her parents had allowed her at their country estate, but this would have to do for now.

This room would remain private. Freddie wasn't ashamed of her odd hobbies, but she knew most of the *ton* would be unable to understand any of her interests. They were quirky even for a man, let alone the daughter of an earl or now the wife of a viscount and future marquess.

Miles had been true to his word of leaving her alone. They had been married two weeks now, and she had hardly seen him. At dinner, they sat at opposite ends of the long table, not saying a word to one another. Freddie had attempted conversation with him, but he had either ignored her or merely grunted in response.

During the days they kept to themselves, each busy with their own pursuits, though what Miles did, Freddie was unsure. It seemed he helped look after some of his father's estates, as he spent much time conversing with his man-of-business and sending correspondence.

At night... well, at night, Freddie waited.

He hadn't yet come to her. Not once. Not on their wedding night, nor any night thereafter. She waited with great anticipation, though whether it was nerves or excitement that had coursed through her veins, she wasn't entirely sure — they were both rather closely connected. She was tempted to ask Miles what had kept him away. It wasn't like her to leave it alone, but she also wasn't entirely sure just what she was supposed to say.

Miles, dear, I was just wondering why you haven't come and made love to me yet?

Even Freddie couldn't say that. Especially because she feared what the answer might be — that Miles hadn't come to her because he had no attraction to her, no wish to be with her in that way.

She had sat on the bed, both expectant and excited that first night. Then she became annoyed that he was making her wait. Until, finally, her anger began to simmer when she realized he wasn't coming at all.

The next night, she had left the door between their chambers slightly ajar so that he would be more than aware she was open to him coming to her.

He still had not arrived.

That was when Freddie knew something was wrong. Yes, they might be together in name only, but there were plenty of loveless arranged marriages all over England. They still required heirs. Besides that, even if they did not love each other, that didn't mean they couldn't find some pleasure with one another, did it?

Freddie was tempted to raise the subject with her friends, or perhaps even one of her sisters, but she couldn't bring herself to do so. She was too embarrassed, for there was clearly only one answer. Miles didn't want her.

"How is marriage treating you?" Jemima had asked with interest the last time they had taken tea together.

Freddie had smiled as she had for two weeks now, portraying the front that appeared to the world.

"Oh, just as I always would have hoped," she said truthfully. For this was what she *had* hoped. Only now that she was married, it was no longer what she wanted.

She was lonely. And she wanted to feel her husband's touch upon her.

She watched him when he wasn't aware of it. Whether it was across the table at dinner, or the odd time she would see him in the corridors of the house. His brow seemed to be continually furrowed, as though he lived in deep concentration, though upon what, Freddie could only guess. He wasn't a particularly statuesque man, but he was lean in all of the right ways. And those moments when his eyes rose to meet hers, Freddie was always startled by just how bright and vibrant they were, as though they could pierce right through her.

But still, he had no time, no thought for her.

So she continued to work. She had an idea, one that seemed silly, but if she could get it right…

"What are you doing?"

She squealed at the voice from the door and jumped up from the table she was currently working at. Her heart remained at its quickened pace when she saw her husband within the door frame.

"I'm puzzling over something," she said as she placed a hand on her chest, as though she could rub her heart rate back to its regular beat.

"What would that be?"

"Oh, nothing," she said, her cheeks reddening. She had no

idea if her fleeting thought would ever come to anything, and she would prefer not to explain the idea to Miles, for he would likely think she was wasting her time.

"Tell me," he said, his voice soft but slightly commanding, and she widened her eyes at him as she nibbled her lip, determining whether or not she should comply.

He sat in a chair next to her workspace and waited. Freddie remembered one thing from when they were children — Miles was patient. He had once sat for an entire day in front of an owl's burrow, just waiting for a glimpse. If she wanted to continue her work uninterrupted, she would have to give him some information.

"I am working on candlelight," she finally said, and he cocked his head in supposed interest.

"Candlelight?"

"Yes," she confirmed. "You and I… we are fortunate that our wax candles last longer than the tallow most use. I believe there may be a way to extend the time each candle burns. It would help in so many ways. Servants wouldn't have to change them as often, or in families less fortunate, they would have fewer candles to buy. More light could be projected into the home. Which would be wonderful, especially during the dreary winter months."

"Huh," was his response, and Freddie wasn't sure if that was his way of proclaiming interest or confusion. "How does it work?"

"Well," Freddie began, "it's not the candle itself, but the candlestick. You see…."

Unlike most people, Miles was looking at her intently as she spoke. Although it was strange, she thought, for she realized that he wasn't so much looking into her eyes as most people would, but rather… he was watching her mouth.

Freddie rubbed her lips and chin with the back of her

hand. Had a piece of her noon meal been left on her face? Was that what he was staring at?

"Can you say that again?" he asked and she nodded, repeating herself, though now she was distracted by whatever it was he was staring at. He was leaning into her now, his eyebrows furrowed.

"I see," he said, but she could tell he had no idea what she was talking about. "It's an interesting idea, Freddie. You're very talented."

"Thank you," she said as he turned to go.

Freddie eyed his retreating back. Something had been nagging at her, that she couldn't get out of her mind. Now it had twigged again.

"Miles," she said softly, but he didn't respond.

"Miles," she said a bit louder, and still he didn't turn.

"Miles!" she practically shouted, and he paused for a moment, his head tilting as though something had captured his attention, but he continued out the door.

Freddie crossed her arms over her chest as she watched him go, the truth now as clear as could be.

Miles was deaf.

* * *

MILES SAT IN HIS STUDY, alone but for the tall glass of amber liquid before him. Alone by choice, he thought glumly as he dropped his head into his hands and rubbed at the ache beginning to form.

The pain typically began close to the end of the day, when all of the concentration of reading lips and listening for the small hints of sound took its toll.

He could go upstairs, enter his wife's bedchamber, and find a way to bring himself relief. He knew she was waiting for him —

he had seen the open door, had managed to look in far enough to see her sitting on the edge of the bed, as beautiful as could be with her long, glossy, chocolate hair plaited and hanging over her shoulder, down the front of her lacy white night-rail which he found as attractive as any ball gown ever could be. Her fingers had toyed with the end of the plait, tantalizing him.

But he couldn't go in.

To go in would mean solidifying their marriage. It would be showing the vulnerable side of himself. In the darkness, he wouldn't know anything she said, would expose him and likely give up his secret.

But even more frightening was the thought that if he went to her, he could, in all likelihood, lose his heart.

What would she think of him, knowing who he was and what he hid from her? He'd rather their life remain as it was — that she be angry with him, frustrated that he wasn't giving her any more than he was, that he hadn't been a true husband to her.

This is what she wanted, he told himself as he finally rose from the desk, downing the brandy before replacing the decanter in the cabinet where he kept all of his spirits. She wanted a husband in name only. Someone who would look after her, give her his name, and ensure that she could live the life she wanted.

He knew she had likely expected that, at the very least, they would live as husband and wife. The truth was, he had expected it as well. But it was proving so much more difficult than he would have thought.

For he could finally admit to himself, even if he couldn't go to her, that he wanted her. He wanted her with an ardor that he could barely control. She was beautiful, there was no denying that. She was also exuberant, passionate, and intriguing — everything he was not. She was intelligent, though she made sure not to come across as superior to anyone else.

He was drawn to her in a way that he nearly could not describe.

It didn't matter, Miles told himself as he made for the door. He lifted a candlestick on his way by the desk, smiling as he did so, for it reminded him of Freddie and her idea. An interesting one to be sure. He didn't completely understand it — he might have, if he had actually been able to pay attention to her words, but he was rather too captivated by the enthusiasm with which she had been describing her thoughts. She wasn't very big, but when she spoke, she used her entire body, becoming much grander than one could ever imagine.

The smile remained on his face as he opened the door, taking a step into the corridor—

And right into his wife.

CHAPTER 9

"*O*of!"

Freddie bounced off of Miles, nearly falling to the floor, but he quickly shot out an arm and caught her before she landed. He pulled her up forcefully enough that she fell into his chest, his arm not holding the candlestick wrapping around her back.

"Freddie!" he exclaimed before stepping back to look at her — whether to assess her for injury or to better be able to hear her, Freddie wasn't entirely sure. He must read lips. She had pondered what she had discovered all afternoon since he had left her workspace. Everything made so much more sense now. Why she always thought he was ignoring her. Why he was always looking at her. Why he spoke so infrequently.

She wondered how *much* he could hear. She sensed that he had some hearing, for otherwise how could he follow along while dancing, or hear sounds that would allow him to turn at various moments?

There was much to learn about him, but first she had

some important questions — why hadn't he told her, and was he ever planning to say anything?

"What are you doing?" he asked her now, and she shrugged.

"I couldn't sleep."

"So you decided to walk the corridors?"

"Is there something wrong with that?" she arched an eyebrow. "This is my home too, isn't it? I can do as I please."

"Yes," he said with a nod. "I suppose that is true."

"Where would you prefer I be?" she asked, unable to help slightly provoking him. "Upstairs, waiting for you?"

While Freddie couldn't clearly see him in the dim light, she had a feeling that his cheeks were now bright pink. She was attempting to speak as loudly and clearly as possible without him suspecting what she was doing, and he had obviously ascertained what she had said.

"Now, Freddie—"

"It's all right, Miles," she said, taking a step back from him. "I shouldn't have said such a thing. Sometimes I speak before I think too hard on what it is that I'm about to say."

"It isn't your fault," he muttered, placing a hand on the small of her back and escorting her down the corridor. Was he going to lead them upstairs? Freddie's pulse began to flutter in anticipation.

But no. He stopped at his study door at the far end of the hall, ushering her in. He lit one of the wall sconces, and light filled the small room that was lined with floor-to-ceiling bookshelves, which were brimming with indiscrimate books of a wide variety.

Freddie was caught between disappointment that they were not going upstairs together, and relief that he had not simply abandoned her to her own chambers. She couldn't return to her lonely bedroom, knowing that he was but a room away. This man she had thought she knew so well had turned out to be a stranger to her, and she needed more from him.

"What has you awake so late?" she asked after he had shut the door behind him and moved deeper into the room, closer to her as the fire cracked in the corner.

"I have never been able to sleep much," he said, one side of his lips curling as though he had confessed a great sin. "Sleep eludes me until after the clock strikes twelve, no matter the evening. It's rather troublesome."

"What do you do?" she asked, genuinely interested. His father was still the marquess, so he would have little responsibility. As far as she knew, he didn't spend much time out at clubs. If he did, he had been quite discreet about it.

"I…" he hesitated, leaving Freddie with the thought that he had been contemplating sharing something with her, but he had, instead, held back. "I read, mostly," he said, and Freddie nodded, remembering him as a young lad, always hidden somewhere with a book in hand. "But I also do some work, for I have begun to oversee some of my father's work. He isn't exactly keen on the thought, but he has little choice, for like it or not, it will be mine to take on someday."

Freddie frowned.

"Why wouldn't he like it? You are his eldest son."

"Much to his chagrin," Miles said with a snort. "Let's just say that my father has never quite… understood me. He would far rather that Benjamin was his heir, but there is little he can do about it, save end my life."

"Miles!" Freddie gasped in shock. She had sensed the tension between Miles and his father, but he couldn't truly believe what he had just said, could he? It was ludicrous.

"I am jesting," he said, though his words were hard and cold, a far cry from a jest. Freddie stared at him, attempting to see beneath the surface of his frozen features to learn more. He was so difficult to read, to even guess what he might be thinking. She wished he would open up just a bit, to let her in to learn more. But he turned from her, causing her some anguish, for she knew that he was not only hiding from her but disinterested in whatever she might be wanting to say.

He took a seat on one of the Chippendale embroidered chairs, crossing his ankle over his knee as he sat back and looked at her once more.

"Your work is obviously very important to you," he said, his green eyes boring into hers, causing some disquiet in her soul. His intensity roused something within her, caused her thoughts to wander to what else he might do as fiercely.

When she had entered into the crazy idea of marriage to him, she had thought him *boring* — how wrong she had been. How wrong everyone was about him.

"I am unsure if I would call it work," she said, composing herself and shrugging as she took a seat on the Chippendale brown leather chesterfield across from him, nervously tucking her skirts under her legs, grateful she had not yet changed for sleep. She had been too agitated to consider going to bed, and so had decided to walk off some of her nervous energy — until she had run into Miles. "A hobby might be a better term for it."

"But you have invented things before," he persisted, "things that actually function."

"Yes," she said simply, curious as to where he was headed with his questions.

"Have you patented them?"

"My ideas?" she said with a bit of a laugh. "No."

"Why not?"

"They're just silly ideas that make life slightly easier. No one cares much about them."

"You never know," he said shaking his head. "Besides, they are more than that. Surely you realize it."

"That's kind of you to say," she said, looking down, appreciating his comment yet equally annoyed that his approval was meaning so much to her.

"It's the truth," he said.

"Thank you," Freddie responded softly before a pregnant pause filled the room.

There was so much she yearned to say to him — so many questions to ask, so much that she wanted to tell him about why she did what she did, and what she needed from him — but she couldn't find the words to say anything regarding it all. What if he decided her work was actually somewhat foolish?

He seemed much more at ease with silence, which why Freddie was surprised when he broke it.

"I thought this would mean more to you," he said, his voice somewhat harsh, and Freddie sat up straighter.

"Why would you say that?"

"It was why you married me, wasn't it? So that you could continue all of this?"

Freddie took a breath. He was right, but how could she explain it to him?

"I did say that no one would care about them," she said slowly, her fingertips playing with one another in her lap, her gaze upon them until finally she worked up enough courage to lift it and look him square in the eye. "Except for me. I care. I care very much. I can't explain it. I know it's silly, and trivial, but if I can make something easier for someone, solve an issue, or provide some innovation, it provides me with this feeling of… oh, I don't know, accomplishment I suppose. That I've done something worthwhile. That there is more to my existence than sitting there making polite conversation that has no meaning to it."

"Then you should ensure it is important to everyone," he

said, "and that all know it was you, Fredericka Luxington, who is the genius behind it all."

Fredericka Luxington. The name sounded foreign to her ears — and it was now hers, for the rest of her life. Would it ever become familiar? Would he? Or would both her name and her husband remain strangers to her forever?

"That is lovely of you to say," Freddie said softly, looking down for a moment before returning her gaze to him. His arms were crossed as he leaned back away from her, as though in defense. Freddie longed to be able to go to him, to make him open up and tell her all — but it seemed he considered her the enemy. "Oh, Miles," she sighed. "I am sorry."

"For what?"

"For this. This marriage that you obviously are not particularly interested in. I wish—" Her lip threatened to tremble for a moment, and she caught it between her teeth before it could do so. She took a breath. "I apologize if I, in any way, forced you into this marriage. I wish that you hadn't agreed — hadn't asked me — if you did not want to be with me."

He slowly leaned forward in his chair, his arms untwining as he rested his elbows upon his knees. "Is that what you think?" he asked, raising an eyebrow as his green eyes pierced into her, "That I do not want you?"

Freddie laughed nervously in response. "Well, of course," she said, her voice shaky. "What else am I to think?"

He clasped his hands in front of him, his thumbs rubbing over the backs of his own hands. Freddie swallowed as she wished they were upon her instead.

"Know this," he said, his eyes meeting hers in a silent command. "There is no fault with you. It has all to do with me."

"What are you talking about?" she asked, willing him to tell her, to share his secret with her.

She knew that it would take a leap of faith for him to say

anything. She knew of many people who could not hear who were confined to schools specifically for them. They were said to help, but did they really? She couldn't say she had ever heard of anyone's first-hand experience there.

She knew in some families, people like Miles were often never seen. They were hidden away in the countryside, never to visit London or put a stain on the family's name.

But this was a man who would be marquess one day. Who had managed to pass himself off as a hearing person for so long now that it would be a shock were the secret to come out. He could speak, however, so it was not as though he could be declared an idiot.

Besides, she would never let that happen, she determined. She was his wife now, and while he may be the one who had vowed to protect her, she would do the same for him.

If only he would trust her.

He stared at her blankly, however, before standing and walking toward her.

He leaned over her seat on the Chesterfield, close enough that she could see flecks of gold within the green of his eyes.

His face level with hers, he opened his mouth.

"That is nothing for you to be concerned about," he said. "You live your life, remember? And I live mine."

Then before she even realized what he was doing, he leaned down and pressed his lips firmly against hers. The kiss was brief, over nearly as soon as it had begun, but it was seared upon Freddie's lips, burning now from his touch.

"Goodnight, Freddie," he whispered, his words having finality to them.

By the time Freddie regained her wits to respond, it was too late.

He was gone.

CHAPTER 10

*W*hat had he been thinking?

Perhaps that was entirely the problem, Miles realized. He hadn't been thinking.

No, instead he had acted on instinct. Freddie had looked so small, so sad sitting there on the brown leather sofa, that when she had apologized for seemingly forcing him to marry her, he had seen the despair upon her face, and the apparent worry that there was something about her that was keeping him away.

Which was so very far from the truth.

Then when those plush, pink lips had been so tantalizingly close to his, his body had overcome the restraint he had erected between them and had connected with hers.

Fortunately, he had been of sound enough mind to pull back before it could turn into anything more than a perfunctory kiss.

He had returned to his bedchamber and poured out his pent-up emotion on canvas, as he often did. He had been about to tell Freddie of his late-night hobby but had held back. While it was likely she would have no qualms about it, his father had ridiculed him about it for so long, that he decided it wasn't worth the risk.

He had finally finished the portrait that had tormented him for days, perfecting it after working long into the night, unable to sleep.

Miles ran a hand over his face as he made his way down the stairs to the breakfast table. The townhouse was sizeable, though nothing nearly as grand as the home that would one day be theirs. He just wasn't entirely sure whether he ever wanted to live somewhere his father had called his own. Miles would be waiting for his father to emerge from the grave and tell him everything he was doing wrong.

"Good morning!"

Miles looked up quickly as Freddie's voice cut through his musings. It was, interestingly, strong and clear enough that he knew exactly what she said without having to read her lips.He frowned. Had she done so on purpose? But when he looked up at her, she wore a sweet, endearing smile, and he was unable to question any motives beyond her simple welcome.

"Morning," he said before taking his place at the other end of the table. He hoped she wouldn't attempt any further conversation. They were much too far from one another, but to suggest they sit closer together would be odd without a good reason for it.

"How are you today?" she asked before taking a sip of her tea. Her words were clear and concise, and she held his eye as she spoke. A twinge of nervousness plucked at Miles. She couldn't know — could she?

She smiled at him once more before concentrating on the plate in front of her, and he rose and made his way to the sideboard. He looked over his shoulder a few times to ensure that she wasn't trying to speak to him again, but she was innocently — and silently — eating her eggs and toast.

Freddie looked up at him once more.

"What do you have planned for today?"

Surely she didn't think they would be making any plans together, did she?

"Today?"

"Yes, today," she repeated herself and he shrugged.

"Nothing in particular."

"Have you taken up your seat in the House of Lords?" she asked unexpectedly, and he shook his head.

"I have not."

"Why not?"

Miles shrugged, focused instead on his gratefulness that Freddie's voice carried well. It was a voice he could hear even when he was sleeping; one that stuck with him.

"I have nothing much to offer them."

"Don't be ridiculous," she scolded. "You have plenty to offer them."

"There is already one Luxington present. I am not sure that two are necessary."

It was as close as he would come to telling her that he had no desire to spend any more time with his father than he was already required to.

Freddie, however, was far too perceptive.

"Ah. You are scared of your father."

She tossed the words out flippantly, and he narrowed his eyes at her, for she was too close to the truth — a truth that had caused him much more anxiety than he would ever want to admit to her.

"I am not *scared* of him. I am a grown man."

"I realize that," she softened. "But that doesn't mean that there aren't people — or situations — that we would prefer to avoid."

"Like applying to have your work patented?"

Her eyebrows rose, giving him a better view of those

warm brown eyes that reminded him of hot cocoa on a cold winter day.

"Since when was this about me?"

"Perhaps we should just be done with this conversation."

But she was persistent.

"What do you *do*, then? You have not taken up your seat in the House of Lords, you do not seem to enjoy going out to the clubs, and you have not taken on a great deal of responsibility regarding the estates your father oversees. You must have a hobby of some sort."

He stared at her, attempting to determine whether or not she had a motive for wanting to know more of his daily activities. But her eyes were open, searching, and he was quite sure that she was primarily simply curious.

"I told you… I read."

"Is that all? Nothing else?"

Miles thought for a moment about any reason why he perhaps *shouldn't* share with her his passion. His father had ridiculed him for it once he found out, calling it a lady's pursuit, but his mother had always been quite supportive — though she was in nearly everything he or his brother did.

"Very well," he said, pushing back his chair abruptly. "Come with me."

"Right now?" she asked, astonished. "But I'm only halfway through my breakfast."

"Another time, then," he said, assuming his seat, and to his surprise, she laughed.

"Don't be ridiculous. Show me," she said, standing before asking the footman to leave her plate.

He nodded, his heart hammering as he walked down the corridor. He led her up the stairs and down the corridor, not looking back until he stopped in front of the door. He glanced over at her.

"We are going to your chamber?" she asked, her eyes

wide, and he couldn't help but smile at her attempt to mask her nervous interest.

"We are," he said, pushing open the door.

His room, which attached to hers through their dressing rooms, was open and airy, with a window that faced the green across the street — exactly why he had chosen this space for his work. That, and the solitude. Miles walked over to the window. There sat his stool, and, in front of it, a covered easel. He hesitated for a moment before lifting the sheet. Very few people had ever seen his work. His mother, of course, and his brother. His mother was always complimentary, but she would be with everything he did. His brother enjoyed it, but he didn't spend a great deal of time waxing poetic — Benjamin far preferred beautiful objects that were living and breathing, who he could charm and seduce.

Miles took a breath and exposed the canvas. He closed his eyes for a moment, not wanting to look at Freddie, but then he couldn't help his need to view her reaction.

"Oh, Miles!" Freddie gasped. "This is… this is…"

"Please," he held up a hand, "you do not need to say anything. It's a hobby, really, is all, and I'm only sharing because you were curious. I do not need false compliments."

"But Miles," she said, turning from the canvas to him, and back again. "This is beautiful. *Stunningly* beautiful. You've taken the green beyond and turned it into… a masterpiece."

Miles hadn't been aware of just how much her approval would mean to him. How he had longed to see in her face, at the very least, some interest in what he did. It scared him, how much she mattered in such a short time.

"Thank you," he said softly, before replacing the cloth. "It is not quite finished yet."

She turned to him with shining eyes, walking over and placing her hands on his shoulders. He started at her touch.

"Miles, you must do something with these paintings. Showcase them. Send them to galleries. At the very least, we must hang them in our own home!"

He laughed ruefully. "That is kind of you, Freddie, but completely unnecessary. There are far greater masters available to hang on our walls."

"There are none like this," she said, shaking her head, "and what could possibly mean more than work from your own hand?" She cocked her head as she studied him. "You are not… ashamed of this, are you?"

"Of course not," he blustered, but as always she saw through him.

"Why do you hide up here, then?"

"I like the view."

"The same view exists on the floor below in the drawing room."

"That is your space," he said, stepping back, away from her touch, "for visitors and such."

"Oh, Miles," she laughed. "The drawing room is *our* space. One in which I believe an original Miles Luxington painting should be showcased."

"We shall see about that," he said, but her words warmed him through, and he had to fight the smile that threatened to emerge.

She walked over to the easel before glancing back at him. Her fingers came to the canvas.

"Miles, you have more paintings beneath here. Can I see—"

"No!" he exclaimed, surging forward to attempt to stop her from looking behind. But he was too late. They both stopped and stared at the painting before them.

For there, staring back at them, was Freddie herself.

Miles shut his eyes for a moment before opening them with trepidation. What would she think? He had painted her the way she had looked the night of the ball at Wyndham House. She had been dressed in a cream dress with red piping, her hair piled on her head. Last night he had made the smallest of additions to finally capture her small half-smile, with the crinkle of her eyes that looked to be nearly winking at him, as though she was sharing a joke with whoever she was looking at.

Miles was typically more critical than complimentary regarding his own paintings, but as he had stared at this one night after night, taking in her beauty, he thought he had done a fairly decent job.

He didn't usually mind silence. It was, after all, what he lived day after day. But the stillness that filled the air between them now contained an undercurrent of emotion that he couldn't accurately describe. One of anticipation, revelation, and surprise.

"You painted me."

Miles could just barely hear her words but accompanied by her expression, they were shocked. He didn't know what to say to her.

"I, ah, didn't mean for you to see that," he said, running a hand through his hair. "I wanted to do a portrait, and you were a… convenient subject."

He thought he caught a hint of sadness as she looked at him, the small smile lifting her lips tinged with regret. Had he said the wrong thing?

"I was convenient?" she murmured, at least, he thought she did as her voice was low. "You have quite a memory, Miles, for I never once posed for you."

No, she hadn't. She didn't need to, for her face was burned in his mind. He yearned for her with all of his being. As her husband, he was well aware that he could have her whenever he chose — but the truth was, he was scared.

It was not his father he was afraid of. His father, however, had taught him to fear rejection, to push love away for the thought that should someone know his truth, they would think him as mad as his father did.

He didn't think Freddie would. But one could never be sure...

Freddie reached out and brushed her fingers over his sleeve. He had been so caught up in his musings, his assumptions on what she might think after seeing this, that he had averted his gaze. Had she been speaking to him? He couldn't be entirely sure.

Her cheeks were flushed, her eyes glistening with moisture. Was she... crying?

"Miles," she said before clearing her throat. "Thank you. Convenient or otherwise, that is the nicest thing anyone has ever done for me."

"The painting?" he asked, confused.

She nodded, and to his surprise and dismay, a tear ran down her face.

"Why are you crying?" he asked, having no idea how to comfort a tearful woman.

"Because," she said, wiping away the drop of moisture. "It's beautiful. I had no idea that you thought so highly of me."

"It's just a painting," he said with a shrug, somewhat embarrassed, but before he could think any further on her reaction, she rushed into his arms, lifted her face, and pressed her lips against his.

CHAPTER 11

*F*reddie sensed Miles stiffen at her touch, and mortification coursed through her at her impulsive action. She removed her hands from his neck to push herself back away from his chest, but he surprised her by catching her hands in his, his fingers encircling her wrists. He held her there, flush against him, as he matched the pressure of her lips.

They stood there, statues for a moment, until he began to slowly move his lips over hers, as though experimenting, to see how she would react.

What he couldn't know was how the smallest of movements on his part were causing explosions of fire within her.

Freddie, unfortunately, was no innocent, but she was unprepared for the onslaught of emotion a single kiss could cause.

His chest was warm beneath her fingertips, his hands strong around her bare skin. His kiss spoke of everything he had never put into his words. Words, it seemed, did not come easily to him, but she had seen his feelings through the brush strokes on that canvas. Once she had begun to study it, she had come to the stunning realization that he cared for her. It was that revelation that had caused tears to spring to her eyes, leading one to fall down her face. She had been so fearful that her husband had nothing but regret regarding her, and yet he had painted her with such likeness, such care, that she had been utterly flabbergasted.

She had acted on impulse, needing to show him in the only way she could determine how, that she felt the same — that she wanted him with an ardor that did not seem to have any inclination of cooling.

That he was returning her kiss with such equal passion caused that warmth to begin melting away the iciness that had existed between them since the wedding. It was a thawing, a beautiful promise of what could await.

Until he stepped back away from her.

"I'm sorry."

"What?" she gasped.

"I shouldn't have kissed you like that."

"Are you mad?" she asked, to which he started as though he had been slapped in the face.

"What if I was?"

"Mad?" she asked, confused. "Miles, that is just a figure of speech."

"So you think," he muttered, and Freddie was completely baffled. One moment he was promising to be a passionate lover, the next he was the ice king once more. What had she said? All she had asked was if he was… oh. The realization washed over Freddie, rendering her warm with embarrassment. She had heard of people who couldn't hear being rendered deaf, dumb, or — perhaps — mad. But who would have ever said such a thing to Miles? He didn't truly believe that, did he?

"Miles," she said, attempting to explain, "I only meant that you have confused me. One moment you are interested, the next you seem to want nothing to do with me. I hardly know what to think."

"I know, Freddie, and I'm sorry," he said with a sigh as he ran a hand through his hair once more. "I haven't been entirely... attuned to your feelings and I apologize for it."

"Thank you," she said, though she remained somewhat perplexed by his ever-changing emotions. "What do you say we get out of this house tonight? We've received many invitations."

"I don't think so," he said, shaking his head before she had even finished her sentence.

"Why ever not? It would be fun. A dinner party, perhaps? Or a ball?"

"I would dread both."

Freddie bit her lip. She could understand why he might, as each called for conversation that would likely prove difficult for him.

"We could spend most of the night dancing," she suggested. "What do you think?"

"I think not."

"The theatre?"

"No."

She sighed. She had no desire to be relegated to this house forever — particularly if her husband ignored her half the time.

"Please, Miles? Will you think about it?"

If only he would share his secrets with her, then she could help him when they were out.

She gave him her most pleading stares, to which he finally resigned.

"Fine," he finally said with a groan. "Choose your party, and we will go."

Freddie smiled triumphantly. They would have a good

time — she would make sure of it. For she would help him in whatever he needed – even if he hadn't asked for it.

* * *

"REMIND me who these people are again?"

Miles leaned in close to Freddie to whisper in her ear as they stood inside the foyer awaiting their opportunity to greet their hosts. He was rewarded with tendrils of her hair tickling his cheek as her scent of orange blossoms washed over him.

Every day it was becoming harder and harder to resist his wife. She was the most beautiful little package he had ever laid eyes on, and the fact he knew that she was his — in name, at least, if nothing else — made her even more enticing.

"Mr. and Mrs. Keswick," she said with a shrug of one delicate shoulder underneath her heavy cloak. "I must confess that I have forgotten their given names, if I ever knew them. They are the parents of Celeste Keswick, who is a dear friend of Jemima's."

"Ah, one of your circle, then."

He knew that there was one appointment his wife kept weekly, and that was tea with three of her friends. He had passed the drawing room one day while they were all within and he had been rewarded by the sound of her unreserved laughter, which he had never heard in his own presence.

"I suppose you could say that," she said with a nod.

"Tell me, what does Miss Keswick do?"

"Do?"

"Why, yes. You all seem to 'do' something — something unconventional that were you to mention to any other young woman you would be disdained. Wyndham waxes on about how creative his wife is, and that she designed the entirety of his house. You have your inventions. Miss St. Vincent is known throughout the *ton* for the potions she creates. Half of them think her a witch."

"Jemima is not a witch!" she said in such great defense of her friend that Miles was nearly jealous she felt so passionate about another.

"I obviously know that," he replied, rolling his eyes. "But I cannot say the same about most others."

Freddie sighed, clearly not particularly in favor of the opinions of most of her peers. Miles agreed with her.

"So?" he continued. "Miss Keswick?"

"Ah, yes," she said. "Celeste... she enjoys searching the stars. An astronomer of sorts."

"An astronomer?"

"Yes," Freddie said with a bit of a laugh. "I will never understand it myself. The thought of such an unknown expanse gives me a bit of trepidation, if I'm being honest. But she loves it all. I don't understand half of what she is talking about."

"I would have to say I agree with your sentiments."

They shared a smile, one that warmed Miles, as Mr. and Mrs. Keswick awaited them and Miles had to concentrate — on them, as well as any other conversations to come.

It wasn't so difficult to get through nights like these, but it pained him to do so without a break. Sometimes if his mother was with him, it helped him as she would ensure he was aware of who was speaking to him and what they were saying, but he could hardly attend each social event with his mother. If only Freddie knew. He looked her way and she smiled at him — would she continue to smile that way at him if she knew the truth?

They continued on past the line, making their way through the ballroom.

"Oh, there is Rebecca and the Duke," Freddie said, turning her head back to him, and he nodded his head.

"Would you like to go see them?"

"First, I think I would like a dance," she said with a smile.

Miles looked at the dance floor, dismayed to find that it was nearly empty. It seemed that it was far too early in the ball for there to be much participation.

"Not now, Freddie," he said, shaking his head, and he saw her smile fall ever so slightly. Would he ever stop being the one to cause her unhappiness?

"Very well," she said, pushing the smile back upon her face. "Perhaps a drink, then?"

He nodded, relieved to have something to do besides stand around and converse with the other couples. He was halfway across the room when he realized that he had no idea what Freddie liked to drink. He tried to think back to any previous occasions, but he had been remiss in paying any attention to what she had availed herself of.

Perhaps lemonade, then, and whiskey for himself.

He was halfway back across the room with drinks in hand when he noticed that his wife was no longer with the duke and duchess. Nor was she with Jemima, who was not far from her brother. Where in the...

There she was. In the middle of the ballroom with Lord Essex. The baron was staring down at her with a wide grin on his face, which Freddie returned as they laughed about something, though what, Miles would never know.

Anger began to churn in his belly before he realized it was more than anger. He wanted to stride across the ballroom, place his hands on Essex, and rip him off of his wife. He wanted to tell Freddie that he didn't want to see any other man touching her but him. He wanted— but as his fingers tightened on the sweating glasses within his hands, one tiny thread of logical thought began to emerge through the red that clouded his vision.

It didn't matter what he wanted anymore. For he could have been the one dancing with Freddie. He could be the one going to bed with her every night. But he had chosen not to. Every time he told her "no," every time he stared at the now-closed door between their chambers, he was pushing her away, leading her to accept the dance of another. How long would it be before she chose to be with another as well? She was warm, fiery, and friendly. She wouldn't be satisfied with a life of coldness, living with the wall he had built between them.

A hand clapped his shoulder and he turned to find the Duke of Wyndham staring at him with an eyebrow cocked over his piercing, assessing blue eyes.

"Something bothering you, man?" he asked knowingly as he flitted his gaze out onto the dance floor at Freddie. "I called your name a few times, but you were so intent on whatever it is you were watching that you must not have heard me."

"My apologies," Miles said. "Yes, I was... concentrating."

"It's never easy watching your wife in the arms of another," Wyndham said gruffly. "Even if it is but a friendly dance. The *ton* and their ridiculous rules. I say stuff them all."

Miles chuckled, some of his anger diffused by the duke's refreshing words.

"Here comes your wife now," Wyndham said, pointing with his chin, and Miles turned to find Freddie walking toward him, escorted by her dance partner. He steeled his jaw as he mechanically handed her the lemonade, which she eyed distastefully. One more thing he had just learned about his wife.

"Miles, do you know Lord Essex?" she asked, her smile faltering as though she could tell something was wrong.

Miles looked over his shoulder to see that Wyndham had left them.

"I do," he said with a curt nod. He didn't know him well, but, he had to admit, he seemed an affable enough gentleman. "Essex."

"Gilmore."

They stood there in awkward silence for a moment before Essex, apparently much more gentleman than Miles, turned, bowed over Freddie's hand, and thanked her for the dance before walking away.

Her smile dropped.

"Miles, whatever is the matter with you? You were glaring at Lord Essex as though you were prepared to duel him."

"Perhaps I am," he muttered as he downed his whiskey with nearly one great swallow. He took the untouched lemonade from Freddie's hand before placing it down on one of the tables near them. "Wonderful, another bloody waltz," he said as he saw another prospective dance partner coming Freddie's way. It seemed marriage had only heightened her appeal. Despite her startled glance, he took her hand and began to lead her out onto the dance floor, his mouth set in a grim line as though he was preparing for battle. "Come," he said firmly. "You'll dance with me, now."

CHAPTER 12

*D*espite the fact that Miles was being slightly more heavy-handed than she would have liked, Freddie couldn't help the quickening of her heartbeat at his firm command to her. He hauled her against him, his hand splaying over her back quite possessively. The Keswick's ballroom was, in actuality, two drawing rooms converted for dancing.

Miles closed his eyes for a moment as though it would help him hear the music before he began to lead Freddie through the throng. She had many questions to ask him — why he had been so rude to Lord Essex, why he suddenly had the urge to dance, why he had been glowering with such anger — but she was pressed too close to Miles for him to see her face and she knew he would never hear her over the din of the music and conversation around them. She was too short, the top of her head coming just to his shoulder.

She took a breath, his scent a mixture of clove and mint filling her, providing her a strange sense of calm. Well, if she couldn't speak to him, then she would enjoy this dance with her husband, the one opportunity she had to be near him.

Freddie shifted her hand on his shoulder, tightened the fingers of her other hand around the back of his, in an attempt to tell him with her actions if not her words how much she yearned for his closeness. It was all she could do to keep herself from melting into his body as his breath warmed the top of her ear, tingles beginning to make their way down her spine at the simplest of touches. She stepped close, and the pressure of his hand increased until she was close enough to sense the heat radiating off his body.

The dance was not yet over when he startled her once more by turning from her, placing one hand on the small of her back, and leading her from the room.

"Miles?" she asked, looking up at him, but his gaze was forward, on whatever was their apparent destination. She tugged on his sleeve, and he finally looked down at her. "Where are we going?"

"Away from here," he said cryptically, and Freddie decided to trust him, despite the many glances sent their way as they went. She heard tittering from a group of ladies, with the words "silly inventions" and "not knowing her place" reaching her ears, and she was grateful that Miles could not hear what they said.

He led her down a corridor, where a selection of open doors awaited them. Miles stopped in front of one, looked inside, and then hauled Freddie through the door. The fire was lit within what must be some sort of blue parlor for it was as though someone had taken a bucket full of paint and thrown it over the room. She began to wonder why Miles had brought her to an empty room, but then she was whirled around and pressed back against the wall.

"Miles?" she questioned, her eyes widening at the hunger evident within his green eyes.

"Freddie," was all he said before his head descended, his lips coming down upon hers. His arms slipped around her waist as he drew her closer toward him, holding her flush against him as his lips hungrily slanted over hers again and again.

Freddie could barely think due to the need that coursed through her for more of Miles' touch, more of his demand, more of his fingers which were now skimming over her back to cup her bottom and press her closer to him, allowing her to feel just how much he wanted her. Finally — oh, *finally*, they would be together as true husband and wife.

Freddie couldn't wait.

She wrapped her arms around his neck and opened her mouth to him, whimpering when his tongue slipped inside and began parrying with hers. There was such urgency between them, such tension, that when Miles slipped a hand between them and closed it over her left breast, lightly brushing the nipple, she nearly jumped from his arms at the sensation it caused within her.

She slipped her hands down his neck to grip the lapels of his jacket as she began leading him backward over to the furniture in front of the fire. She didn't know whether it was a chesterfield or a sofa or a settee — she hadn't taken the time to look, and frankly, she didn't much care at the moment. For whatever reason, tonight her husband had decided he wanted her, and she was not going to allow this moment to pass.

They tumbled down onto the piece of furniture — it was blue, she was aware of that much — and Miles trailed his fingers down her side, over her hip, and along her leg through the satiny fabric of her skirts. He had just reached the soft skin of her ankle when he broke away from her with a curse.

"What is it?" she asked, sitting up with him, desperate to keep this connection between them.

"This isn't right," he said, his expression desperate. "Your first time should be on a bed, in your chamber, with all of the comforts that I should be providing you."

Freddie's stomach dropped for a moment, and she nibbled her lip.

"Ah, about that Miles," she said, frustrated that the passion had ebbed enough for her guilty conscience to invade. "This isn't exactly—"

"Come," he said, apparently not hearing her as he took her hand and hauled her up off the sofa. He looked down to assess her condition, taking the care to set a tendril of hair back in place over her ear. The little gesture warmed her heart, and she cautioned herself against reading too much into it. "We are going home."

"Now?" she asked, her heart jumping. They had just arrived, but if he wanted to go home—

"Now."

Freddie eagerly accepted his hand as he led her from the room. He attempted to leave by the end of the corridor, but it seemed it only led to the back of the house. They would have to return through the ballroom.

"Whatever you do," he said, his palm warm through her glove, "do not stop to talk to anyone. We are going home right now, do you understand me?" He glanced at her.

"Perfectly," she said with a smile, enjoying this authoritative side to Miles that she hadn't seen before.

He began to lead them around the outskirts of the makeshift ballroom. They nearly made it to the exit — nearly. They had just come to the entry to the foyer when Miles stopped so suddenly that Freddie ran into his back.

She peeked around him to see just what — or who — could have caused him to halt his progression to the door after his previous stern warning.

It was his father.

* * *

"MILES."

His father stared at him with such contempt that Miles was sure the entire ballroom could feel the hatred that existed between the pair of them. Miles nodded at him curtly as all of the ardor that had overtaken his reasoning and compelled him to the door faded away, as though his father had taken a bucket of cold water and poured it over top of him.

"Father."

"Leaving so soon?" his father sneered, and Miles shrugged.

"What business is it of yours?"

He sensed Freddie look sharply at him out of the corner of her eye, and Miles realized that she had likely not seen much interaction between the two of them and therefore wouldn't have known that such animosity existed. Well, she would now.

"It is my business when my heir, who has sequestered himself away for most events, decides that he wants to return to society."

Miles took a breath, preparing his reply, but Freddie stepped up next to him, tucking her hand around his arm possessively.

"It was my idea to come," she said, holding that small, pointed chin up defiantly. "And we are having a fine time."

"Then why leave?" his father asked, eyebrows raised as an evil smile stole across his lips while he addressed Freddie. Miles wanted to jump in front of her and tell his father to desist talking to her, but for what reason would he have to do so? "Is it because Miles here is a social disgrace, or is it because the rumors are true and all of the *ton* is talking about you?"

"What do you mean?" Miles said, his head whipping around to her, and she pressed her lips tightly together.

"Some of the women of the *ton* know of my... unconventional hobbies. They find it rather entertaining to speak of."

Miles' anger flared once more at the thought of anyone making light of his wife, especially that it was due to what set her apart and showed the intelligence she possessed, unlike so many of these empty-headed misses.

"Or perhaps another piece of information has come to their attention."

Unease churned within him. What could his father be on about?

"It seems that a certain earl has loose lips. He has shared some delicate information with me."

Miles looked over at Freddie to see if she was aware of just what his father was speaking of and was taken aback by her expression. Her face had gone white, her pink lips and brown eyes pronounced in contrast.

"What is he talking about?" he demanded, suddenly needing to know what it was that would so frighten her — and so entertain his father. This could not be good. "Freddie?" he urged, no longer caring about his father, who laughed.

"Oh, Miles," he said. "You always did know how to choose unwisely. Such as your foray here tonight. Stay home from now on."

With that warning, he walked away, leaving the two of them staring at each other.

"Miles," Freddie said quietly before dipping her head and saying something he couldn't hear.

"What was that?" he asked, his fingers coming to her chin

to tip her head up toward him so that he could see her lips once more.

"I asked if we could go home."

"Of course," he said, before calling for the carriage.

He would do as she wished and take her home.

But he was not letting this go. Not after they had come so far.

CHAPTER 13

*I*t was a terse, silent carriage ride home. There was no light within, so Freddie knew she couldn't say anything, for Miles might not be able to hear her. He didn't ask. She wondered if he would. She had the feeling, however, that this, he would not let go.

Finally, they arrived home. Miles helped her down out of the carriage, but rather than the mad dash up to their chambers that she had envisioned, instead it was a slow climb of the stairs, both of them dreading what was likely to be a difficult conversation.

Miles led them to her chamber, much to her surprise, though Freddie appreciated the gesture. Here was a place of comfort, where she would feel more at ease as she told her story. She had no idea how Miles would react.

She only wished that she had been able to tell him this in her own time.

Instead of nearing the bed, they sat in the chairs that were by the fireplace in her room. Freddie actually had never sat here before, having had no one in her chamber to converse with.

They each took a chair, and Freddie twisted her hands nervously together. Miles said nothing, instead sitting back in his seat and waiting for her to begin.

"I'm sorry, Miles," she said, the only other sound in the room the crack of the fire in the grate, as Freddie spoke loudly enough that he would hear her despite the dim light. "I was going to tell you whenever— when the time came for us to... well." She lapsed into silence for a moment. "You mentioned my first time... making love... but this, in fact, would not be my first time."

He didn't move, though Freddie saw a muscle in his cheek twitch.

"A few years ago, I thought I would be married to an earl of my parents' choosing. He courted me. Carriage rides through Hyde Park, dances together at balls, that sort of thing. Then one night... things got carried away." She squeezed her fingers together. "He... he took me in the gardens at Lord Hollingsworth's annual ball."

Miles stiffened.

"He *took* you? Did you..." His voice was like steel. "Did you not want him to?"

Freddie dipped her head for a moment, shame flooding through her. "I— I accepted his kiss, and his touch at first. But I didn't want to do... that. Not then. I told him no, but he said that he... didn't hear me. He apologized afterward, said that he thought it was what I wanted."

"But you didn't."

"No."

Miles rose and paced over to the fireplace, his fingers grasping the shelf above, his knuckles white.

"Who was it?"

He turned to see her answer.

"It doesn't matter."

"Who. Was. It."

"Lord Lovelace," she whispered. "But please, Miles, it doesn't matter."

"What happened to the two of you?" he asked, his words forced out as his fists clenched at his side.

"I told my father I wouldn't marry him. I refused to spend my life with such a man. Luckily, my father accepted my decision and didn't ask any further questions."

"And then?"

"Then he married another. I think they were a love match. She seems happy enough. No revenge is necessary, Miles. All I ask for is forgiveness."

"Forgiveness?"

Freddie brushed away the tears that began to form in her eyes. "I should have told you — especially before we married. I was going to, before we came together. I just... it's so shameful. I didn't know how to share such a thing. And, if I am being honest... I didn't want you to reject me."

Miles re-took his seat, leaning over to take Freddie's fingers in his.

"Freddie," he said, his voice so gentle that it actually startled Freddie, who looked up at him.

"Yes?"

"There is nothing to forgive. It isn't your fault. And even if you had wanted his touch, well, you don't anymore, and that is what matters."

Tears began to fall from Freddie's eyes. She would never have imagined that he would be so understanding, so forgiving. It was more than she could ever have asked for.

"Thank you, Miles," she said, to which he only nodded.

Then he opened his arms, and Freddie nearly jumped from her chair to go willingly into them.

* * *

MILES HAD THOUGHT this evening would end much differently.

It was strange, however. Somehow, his wife curled up in his lap, her head upon his chest as he stroked her hair while tears fell from her eyes, was more intimate than any other act could ever be.

He hoped she had been able to find a release of sorts from sharing with him. She seemed much more at peace, at any rate.

Miles, on the other hand?

He was still burning with need, but of an entirely different sort. He had the need to find Lovelace and challenge him a duel to restore his wife's honor. He would use whatever necessary — pistols, swords, fists — to seek justice for Freddie.

Miles looked down at her sleeping in his arms, her long black lashes resting on her cheeks, her dark hair lying over his chest.

Except... it wasn't what she wanted. He knew that, and yet... he would do what he could, if only it didn't mean sullying her name as well. But if he challenged Lovelace, that was what would happen. All would know of the two of them, and her name would be muddied, even though it was not at all her fault.

He couldn't do that to her.

He ran a hand up and down the soft skin of her arm, remembering what it was like to hold her in his arms earlier that evening. Of how she had yearned for him just as much as he had longed for her.

Perhaps this had been a sign, he thought ruefully, leaning his head back on the chair behind him. For the truth was, he was becoming far too invested in his wife. He cared so much that he knew it would only hurt all the more if she rejected him.

He craned his neck to look at her face, but then a snore erupted from her, loud enough that even he heard it in the hushed room, and he couldn't help but laugh. How could such a noise come from someone so small? He lifted her effortlessly as he walked across the room and laid her down on the bed, tucking the blankets around her. He supposed she would like to change into her nightclothes at some point, but she could do that when she woke — for if he attempted to do so, it would only end in embarrassment for both of them.

She nuzzled her head into the pillow, as though she was searching for the chest her cheek had previously lay upon, but she remained in sleep. Miles took the opportunity to look around the room. It had been some time since he had been within. She had taken the pink-flowered motif and added some of her own accents. There was a vase full of peonies and roses on the vanity table, while a lace coverlet lay over the top of the bed.

He smiled. For a practical, inventive woman, she also seemed to love all of the extra frills one would ascribe to a more flippant woman. Whether it be lace on her dresses or ribbon wound through her hair, she loved beauty around her. It was an interesting combination, and one uniquely her.

As he left the room, softly shutting the door between them, he tried to fight the knowledge that despite the fact he was able to force himself to leave, his heart remained in the room with his wife.

"FREDDIE?"

Freddie jumped up, startled, her cheeks immediately filling with heat when she saw who was at the door to her workshop.

The table in front of her was piled high with books as well as sketches of an idea she had. Most of the morning had been taken up with research. She was going to solve Miles' problem for him. She just had to figure out how.

"Miles," she greeted her husband, quickly covering the material on the table in front of her, not wanting him to see what she was working on — at least, not yet. "How are you this morning?"

She had to admit that she had been relieved when she had missed him for breakfast. She had no idea what she would say to him. What a fool she had made of herself last night. First, she had thrown herself all over him, attempting to lure him back home to seduce him. Then his father had humiliated her, which led to her pouring out her sorrowful story and soaking his clothing with her tears.

And after all of that, he hadn't been the least bit angry with her. She had kept such a secret from him, and he hadn't cared. Hadn't blamed her. Hadn't suggested that she had been a coward for not saying anything to him sooner.

How could she hold onto anger at him for not sharing *his* secret with her? Perhaps he had good reason not to. What that reason was, she didn't know, but she would give him time. He deserved that much, at least.

She took a breath.

"Thank you... for helping me to bed last night," she said, nearly unable to meet his eyes.

"How did you sleep?"

"It was one of the best nights of sleep I have had since—in years."

"Good," he said with a small smile as he assessed her, then shuffled his feet, his hands behind his back as he looked around the room. He hadn't spent much time in here. Freddie loved this former parlor near the back of the house. She kept the drapes away from the windows, allowing in plenty of light. Even now, small particles of dust floated through the sunshine, settling themselves on the bookshelves that surrounded the room. It hadn't taken Freddie long to fill them with her own collection of books and curiosities. Miles' gaze wandered over it all before returning to her. "My parents have asked us to dinner tonight."

"Oh, lovely," she said, though she was conflicted. She did enjoy his mother, but none of her limited experiences with his father had been particularly positive. Her father had always put up with Lord Dorrington for her mother's sake, but her father wouldn't be there tonight. However, Miles would be.

"Yes, well…" He ran a hand through his hair. "I tried to decline, but my mother was fairly insistent."

"Perhaps she misses you," Freddie said, understanding more than she wanted to admit, as she thought about how much she would miss Miles if he was ever suddenly far from her life.

She frowned. Where had that thought come from? Miles wasn't going anywhere. Although they did not yet truly feel like husband and wife

"Will it just be the family?" she asked and, after clearing his throat, he nodded.

"Very well," she said with a forced smile. "I will be ready."

CHAPTER 14

*L*ord Dorrington was sitting with one leg crossed over the other on the large sofa in the elaborate drawing room when they entered.

He did not stand at their presence, though his smirk slightly widened. That was not a good sign.

"Miles! Fredericka!" Miles' mother said as she crossed the room and greeted them both with kisses on the cheek. His mother had always seemed to attempt to make up for his father's coldness — though "coldness" was putting it mildly. "Thank you so much for coming. I haven't had the chance to see either of you since the wedding!"

"Forgive me," Miles said, chagrined. He hadn't meant to ignore her.

"Not at all," she said with a smile. "I am pleased you are spending so much time getting to know one another!"

As though he wasn't feeling guilty enough.

If it wasn't for his mother, Miles would never deign to be in the same room with his father. Nor would he ever bring Freddie anywhere near him, especially after the disaster at the ball last night.

As though sensing the animosity now tense in the air, his mother led them over to a sitting area on the opposite side of the room from his father. They made comfortable conversation for a few minutes until another voice rent the air.

"My brother and his bride!"

Benjamin walked into the room, commanding attention, as always, with his good looks and charm. He walked over to them, taking charge of the conversation, complimenting Freddie on how lovely she looked, congratulating her once more on the wedding, asking her questions about her family. When they had been children, it was Benjamin who had spent his days frolicking with Freddie and her sisters, Benjamin who they had gotten on well with, Benjamin who they had followed around with adoring eyes.

Miles loved his brother. Truly he did. But sometimes he wished that he was not so… perfect.

This time when Freddie asked for a drink, Miles paid attention. Madeira. He would remember that. He held his arm out to her when the dinner hour arrived. Despite the fact Freddie was, so far, his wife but in name, he had a strange sense of pride in being the one to escort her through the corridor, hold her chair out for her, and sit next to her at the table.

He noted that Benjamin had been eyeing Freddie with a fair bit of appreciation. While Miles trusted that his brother would never act on such sentiments, he still had the impulse to keep him as far from Freddie as possible.

"Well, this is lovely," their mother said as the footman began to serve. Freddie smiled at her in appreciation while Miles held his breath, praying that this dinner would go far better than most of the other dinners that had been held in this room.

"Yes," his father drolled, an eyebrow raised. Miles could

scarcely hear him, but somehow he knew his tone was laced with sarcasm. "It's been a pity not having Miles about."

"Well," Freddie said pluckily, "I'm afraid I have been stealing all of his attention for my own."

"So tell me, Lady Gilmore," his father said, and Miles' grip tightened around his fork. "What convinced you to marry my son?"

The silence became particularly deafening, and Miles found that his entire family was looking at Freddie with interest. While his father was the only one with the bollocks to ask the question, it seemed that all of them — even his mother — were interested in knowing the answer.

"Miles and I found ourselves to be well suited," Freddie finally said, turning to Miles with an uncomfortable smile. "Marriage between us made sense."

Then there was the part of her wanting a husband she could trust not to control her, but Freddie didn't mention that.

"I always thought Miles here would never marry," his father said now, taking a heaping forkful of roast duck, continuing to speak as he chewed. Miles grimaced. "Thought it would be Benjamin who would carry on the family line."

"I'm happy for them, Father," Benjamin said with an unabashed grin. "You know I'm not keen on all of that responsibility anyway."

His father eyed him with a terse stare.

"You would have done well as my heir, Benjamin," he said, and Freddie looked up with a gasp. Apparently, she hadn't been aware of the extent of his father's ill will toward Miles.

"Benjamin has taken on the responsibility of one of my estates," his father said now, his chest puffing out with pride at the apparent undertaking completed by his younger son.

"Good for you, Benjamin," Miles said, pushing the food around his plate, his hunger vanished. "You are aware,

Father, that I would be pleased to take on more of the responsibilities beyond the one estate I oversee."

His father stared at him for a moment before throwing his head back and laughing.

"Giving you more?" he asked, his eyes widening in incredulity. "Just what would you do with them?"

"Manage them," Miles said quietly. He had no wish to indulge his father by providing him the argument he was looking for, but he did need to begin to learn the tasks that would be presented to him when he would become the marquess one day.

"Oh, Miles," his father said, his face falling as though he actually were melancholic about this situation. "You know that might prove difficult."

"I think not," he countered, but refused to enter into the same argument they had been having for years now with Freddie in the room.

"I'll not have an imbecile running my key estates," his father said, his eyes turning to steel as he stared at his son. Miles said nothing in return this time. Instead, he merely stared down his father as he wondered if he even heard what he was saying anymore, or if he was only trying to raise his ire.

He opened his mouth to retort, but Freddie spoke first.

"Miles is one of the most intelligent men I know," she said, her spine as tall as she could make it, her pointed chin set firmly. Miles' heart warmed at her ready defense.

"Having your wife fight your battles for you, Miles?" his father said, laughing now, though his eyes were cruel. "I suppose there really is nothing you can do alone."

Were his accuser anyone else, Miles would have jumped across the table and defended his honor right there. But there was no way that he could so challenge his father. He preferred avoidance.

He placed his napkin down on the table in front of him.

"I think we are done here."

His mother reached out from her place next to him, resting her hand upon his.

"Please, Miles, don't go," she said, her eyes pleading, "not yet."

She turned to look at his father now, though Miles was aware that no amount of sympathy would emanate from that side of the table.

"Miles would do a fine job, in my opinion," Benjamin said, apparently oblivious to the tension lacing the air.

Miles closed his eyes for a moment, wishing they would all simply stop talking. It seemed as though he had missed part of the conversation — conversation that was centered around him. He was done with it. He and Freddie never should have come here tonight.

"How are people supposed to listen to a man they can't respect?" his father continued.

"What you fail to realize, Father, is that respect and fear are not the same things," Miles said dryly.

"Oh?" his father retorted. "And when they find out their lord is a deaf idiot, just how do you think they'll react? You'll be a laughingstock!"

The world tilted, and surely Miles' heart stopped at his father's words. For all the time he had so carefully hidden his true self from Freddie, his father had shattered the façade with one comment. He closed his eyes for a moment, bracing himself for Freddie's rejection. He knew she would be in disbelief, but how soon would it take her to leave this house, this dinner? She had put up with enough from his father, but now that she knew she was doing so for a man who was not only flawed, but a liar as well…. the wave of humiliation that had been Rosemary's rejection years ago swept over him once more as he finally worked up the courage to turn to look at his wife.

"That is enough!" Freddie stood so suddenly that when she shoved away from the table, her chair went tumbling behind her. His mother jumped, so it must have banged loudly on the floor. Her face reddened when they all regarded her wide-eyed in apparent shock, though Miles could do nothing but stare at his wife, as he seemed to have lost the ability to breath. "Miles is one of the most intelligent, responsible men I have ever met. His tenants will be lucky to have him as their lord."

His father stared at Freddie for a moment before his eyes hardened and his mouth twisted into a cruel smile.

"Why, what a little guardian you have here, Miles," he said slowly. "How quickly she comes to your defense — perhaps because there is much to defend?"

Emotion surged within Miles — nearly uncontrollable anger against his father. He was able to refrain from action, however, because a more powerful emotion made itself known... love.

He loved his wife.

He loved that she didn't pause for a moment at the suggestion that there was something wrong with him. He loved that she would stand up to his father, even though he could sense her trembling beside him. And he loved that she was who she was — creative, passionate, practical, and fiery.

He could never tell her any of that, for once he did it would be crossing to a place of no return, and Miles wasn't sure what the future might hold for them.

He stood and placed his arm around her waist, showing his support for her. Alone it might be difficult to stand against his father, but together... together, he and Freddie could do anything.

"She is right, Father — that is enough," he said, quietly but firmly. "We refuse to listen to this any longer. We are leaving."

"I see now why you had to marry a little harlot like this one," he said as Freddie gasped. "A proper lady would never have married you."

"She is more lady than any man could ever ask for," Miles retorted. "It's time for us to go."

Freddie nodded, placing her hand within his, lacing her fingers through his. She turned from his father, completely ignoring him, and directed her comments to his mother.

"Thank you, Lady Dorrington, for the invitation," she said. "Please know that you are welcome in our home any time."

Miles wondered if her words held more meaning than a simple visit. At his mother's nod, he saw that she understood Freddie's invitation. Miles knew his mother, however. As much as he loved her, she was not strong enough to ever leave. Nor would his father ever likely allow her to. He may not know of love, but he knew of possession.

"I'll walk you to the door," his mother said softly, but his father interjected.

"You will not," he said. "If they choose to go, let them go. They will not interrupt your dinner."

Miles' mother looked at him apologetically, and Miles shrugged as he bent to kiss her cheek.

"Goodnight, Mother," he said, then held his arm out to Freddie, nearly unable to look at her for fear of what he might see. Rejection? Regret? Fear? She may have defended him to his father, but would she be upset that she had chosen to marry him?

But no. As they left the blasted dining room, walking through the wide corridor to the foyer, the only emotion on her face was love reflected back at him.

CHAPTER 15

$\mathscr{F}$reddie took a seat right next to Miles in the carriage. She told herself that it was so he could better hear her, but the truth was, she needed his comforting presence after that exchange with Lord Dorrington, even though it was Miles he had so maligned.

She wondered if Miles would ever have willingly shared his deafness with her. She had hoped that, in time, he would have, but the truth was, she was filled with relief at the fact that it was now in the open and they could face whatever came at them together.

For she understood Miles now, more than she likely ever could have without witnessing such a scene. Growing up with a father like that would cause a person to lose all hope that someone could ever appreciate him for who he truly was.

"I'm sorry about all of that, Freddie," he said, placing his hand over hers where it sat upon his knee. "My father can be rather terrible, but I never would have guessed that he would have gone so far as insulting you."

"That is what you are concerned about right now?" she

said, after placing her hands on his cheeks and turning his head toward her. "Oh, Miles. Your father is a beast. His insults don't bother me. What is truly awful is the fact that he only said them to hurt you. I just... I don't understand what kind of parent would treat his child as such."

Miles snorted. "Mine, apparently. Since the day he realized I was not the perfect heir he wished for, he has done all he can do to lower my esteem."

"I just don't understand it," Freddie said, chewing her lip. "You are his heir no matter what. Nothing could change that. So why not help you rather than hinder you?"

"Perhaps he is plotting my demise," Miles said with a low laugh, but Freddie didn't find it funny.

"Miles—"

But he didn't hear her, couldn't see her in the dark as he had turned away.

"Freddie... I'm sorry I didn't tell you about my condition," he said, looking down at his hands. "I... there was a time, a few years ago, when I was courting another young lady. I had thought to make her my wife."

Freddie had gone silent, and he turned to see that she clenched her hands tightly together. He cleared his throat and continued.

"I shared with her my condition and she... decided that she no longer had any interest in continuing our relationship. I should have told you, Freddie, it wasn't fair to marry you under false pretenses, but... I suppose I just couldn't bear to lose you."

"Miles," she said, her words emerging on a hushed sigh, "we both came to one another with far too much fear over perception, did we not?"

He smiled ruefully. "I suppose that is true. I understand if, now that you know, you wish to continue living our lives as separately as possible."

Freddie reached out, turning his face back toward hers. "Miles, do not be ridiculous," she said purposefully, "I have known about this for days."

"What?" he asked, looking at her so intently she nearly laughed but the moment was far too serious for that.

"A couple of weeks after we married, you were in my workroom," she explained. "I called out to you a few times and you didn't respond. Then it all made sense. I thought you had been ignoring me, but it wasn't that. It was simply that you didn't hear me. It was why you don't like going to balls, as there is so much noise it is likely hard to distinguish anything. I assume you can hear *some* sound?"

He nodded, his eyes glistening in the dim light as they assessed her.

"You are far too intelligent, Freddie."

"Observant," she amended, "and I do much observing of you."

His eyes turned heated at her words, but before she acted upon that thought, she wanted to know more and they hadn't long until they arrived home. Somehow, this cloak of darkness, this carriage with just the two of them, provided a sharing of secrets that might otherwise be impossible.

"Why is your father so…"

"Hateful?"

"Yes."

Miles sighed, taking her hands in his.

"You know, I'm sure, that most often those who cannot hear are considered 'deaf and dumb,' as my father put it. He has always taken so much pride in our lineage that he seems to think of me as a stain upon it. When I was young, two or three I suppose, it soon became apparent that I wasn't speaking, and not only that, not responding to anything others were putting to me. My mother had suspected something was wrong for a time, but she hadn't wanted to inform my father for fear of what he might do. Well, she was right to worry. Initially, he was determined to send me away. Have me live with a distant relative at some estate nowhere near anyone who would have any idea who I was. The only problem was, I was his heir. If it wasn't for my mother, I'm sure he would have faked my death so that Benjamin could inherit. But that was the one thing she wouldn't stand for. If he did such a thing, she told him she would tell everyone the truth, no matter the consequences, and he didn't want to suffer an ill reputation."

His fingers tightened upon hers, and Freddie could sense his tension. She said nothing, however, allowing him to tell his story. She wondered if he had ever told it to another. Likely not.

"As I grew older, my mother realized that I wasn't completely deaf. I worked with her, as well as with a specialized tutor, to determine how to read lips and to focus hard enough when listening that I could learn how to speak. They helped me learn how to determine the volume of my own voice, to put steps to a dance, to function without the ability to hear much of what was around me."

"You've done an admirable job of it," she said, squeezing his fingers. "Most others would never have guessed."

"None of it was good enough for my father. He has hated me since the day he realized I was damaged. I would be fine in giving the title to Benjamin, but it doesn't exactly work like that. If it did, I'm sure my father would have declared me mad by now. But it wouldn't matter — I would still hold the title eventually, just no power."

"He would actually do that? Declare you mad simply because you cannot hear as well as most other people can?" Freddie was incredulous. She had heard of schools for the deaf, of course, but to be declared as *insane*?

"Do you know anyone who is deaf?" he asked, and Freddie pondered his question.

"Well, no," she admitted. "I don't suppose I do."

"There's a reason for that," he said. "Most are sent away to live elsewhere, so they do not tarnish the family name."

"That's ridiculous."

"Not to most," he said. "My father would have followed through with his threat to send me away except for the fact that I told him if he ever did I would tell all of my condition. It would bring too much stain upon the family. No one wants a bit of madness within it."

They were both silent for a moment as they thought on it.

"We don't have to see him anymore," she said, and he nodded in agreement.

"No, we don't."

Freddie had to ask him one more thing, but she wasn't entirely sure how to put it into words. "Miles…"

"Yes?"

"This secret you have been keeping from me, is it… well, is it the reason you haven't come to me? If not— if it is *me*, then I understand. I was simply wondering—"

"Oh, Freddie," he said, turning to her and placing a finger upon her lips to halt her flow of words. "I have wanted to come to you since the day that you entered my house."

"Then why haven't you?" she asked, the breath leaving her on a whoosh as it seemed the air was suddenly sucked from the carriage, for she could barely breathe with him so close in front of her as they spoke on the subject.

"Because I was a coward," he said, his voice nearly breaking. "I was worried you wouldn't want anything to do with me if you knew the truth."

"Then in that," she said with some humor, "you were a fool. For I want you, Miles Luxington. I want all of you. Very, very much."

A low groan erupted from him as Freddie lifted her hands to his face, her fingers grazing over the short bristle upon his cheeks.

"Miles?"

"Yes?"

"Will you make love to me?"

The carriage came to a halt upon her words.

"There is nothing else I would rather do."

Freddie could hardly recall the short journey from the carriage, along the walk, through the corridor, and up the stairs. All she was focused on was *him*. When they reached the landing at the top of the stairs, he picked her up, his scent, a mix of clove and mint, enveloping her. Her heart beat fast as she anticipated what was to come.

Would he be sweet and gentle? Would he be aggressive and passionate? Would he want her to take the lead?

It was funny — as much as Freddie loved being her own woman, of taking charge of her own destiny, in this she needed him to be the one who would show her the way.

It seemed she was not to be disappointed.

Once Miles had her in his arms he strode down the hall, using a hip to open the door to his chamber. A fire danced in the hearth, the dim light just barely pushing back some of the deepest of the darkness of the room. He shut the door behind him with a kick from his booted foot before crossing the dark navy Aubusson carpet to the bed. He lifted Freddie through the canopy and released her so she fell into the soft cloud of his mattress and its covering.

"This is heavenly," she sighed, though, as she had for some time now, she remembered to speak loudly enough that he would hear her.

She was rewarded for her efforts when he grinned wickedly.

"Oh, Freddie," he said with a low chuckle. "We haven't even started yet."

Her heart began to pound so hard she was certain he would be able to hear it as her blood pumped hot through her body. Every nerve was on edge from the tips of her toes up to the roots of her hair as she watched him unhurriedly remove his jacket, followed by his cravat.

Was he not as affected as she? Or even at all?

She tried to sit up to ask, but he lifted a finger and pointed it at her.

"Lie down."

She did so obediently. She had never seen this side of Miles before — she hadn't even known it was there.

But she liked it.

It was as though by sharing their secrets with one another, all the barriers that had been in place between them fell away. That in sharing their innermost thoughts they had opened the door to all of the passion that could exist between them, that had been simmering there since the day they had been married.

If Freddie was not so excited, she would have been relieved.

Apparently, her husband wanted her after all.

Miles threw his cravat to the floor as he crawled over top of her like a cougar stalking its prey. He trapped her head and shoulders between his elbows and forearms before lowering his head to hers.

"Freddie," he whispered, "Are you ready for this?"

"More than I ever have been for anything else in my life," she responded, her eyes meeting his. His pupils were so wide it was as though his eyes had darkened, and when his lips descended upon hers, all of the yearnings that had been building within her for him began to pour through.

She had wondered how his lovemaking would be. Well, it

was simply everything. It began sweetly and gently, but the more she responded, the more his intensity grew. His tongue slipped in to caress hers and when she felt his firm thighs resting between her legs, she rubbed against him greedily, hungrily, which only seemed to fuel him.

"Who are you, Freddie?" he asked in wonder, and she smiled, answering him with her lips upon his.

"Your wife."

CHAPTER 16

*M*iles thought he was already as far gone as any man could be — until Freddie answered with those words.

"Your wife."

She was his. His wife. He might not have been the first to ever be with her, but he would damn well be the last. He kissed her again, drinking her in, wondering if he would ever be able to get enough of her.

He left her lips, kissing his way over the soft skin behind her ear and down her neck. She arched up into him as he did so, and while he wanted to ask her how much she liked it, he didn't want to have to worry about concentrating on what her answer might be.

Right now, he was going to damn well enjoy what he had waited so long for.

He sat back on his heels before taking Freddie's hands and lifting her up so that she was sitting, straddling him. He reached around her, slowly undoing each button on the back of her dress, his fingers caressing the skin they exposed as he loosed each one from its fastening.

Finally, he reached the bottom, and he pushed the creamy satin sleeves off of her shoulders, lifting her arms from them.

"Lie down," he commanded, and when she did as he bid, he grinned in anticipation as he stepped off the bed and worked her skirts down so that the dress slid off her feet. He left it on the floor as he stepped between her legs, placing one hand on each of her bare ankles, running his fingers up her calves.

She jumped slightly at his touch, and power coursed through him at the knowledge that he could evoke such a response from her. Freddie enjoyed leading in most aspects of life — but not in this. He couldn't help himself. In this, he would either take the lead or be equal with his wife.

He was only glad she seemed as pleased with the thought as he.

Miles stood back and stared at her — all of her, nearly completely visible as she was only covered in the thin, soft silk of her chemise.

"Gorgeous," he murmured. "I must paint you like this."

"Right now?" she exclaimed, her eyes widening incredulously, and he laughed.

"Of course not," he said. "Another time. After this. Tomorrow. Next week. Next month. I don't care. But at some point in time, you will be on my canvas — just as you are finally on my bed."

She swallowed hard.

"You wouldn't truly paint me like *this*?" she said, bemused, to which he shook his head.

"Of course not."

She relaxed.

"I would first make you take *all* of your clothes off."

Her eyes widened in shock before a pink stain of embarrassment began to spread out across her cheeks.

"Oh my, Miles," she whispered, and he chuckled once more.

"Your Miles?"

She smiled. "I do like the sound of that."

"Good," he said, before ridding her of all that remained — her stays and chemise, until she was bare before him. She began to scramble backward, reaching for the blanket, but he wagged a finger at her.

"Not now," he said, taking his fill of her, and her brows came together in annoyance.

"It's hardly fair," she said, words which took him a moment to register.

"What isn't?"

"That I should be naked in front of you while you are fully clothed."

"Well," he said with a lazy grin, "if that is all that's bothering you, then go ahead."

He reached his arms out in front of him as an invitation to her, and she hesitantly sat up once more and shuffled over on her knees toward him. She undid his waistcoat before doing the same to his shirt, slipping it off his shoulders so that he was bare down to the torso. He watched her take deep breaths as her eyes ran over him in a path that she followed with her fingers, and he jerked at her touch.

Then her hands came to the top of his trousers and he sucked in a breath. What was she going to do? But Freddie was no coward. She arrived at his fall and she undid it, although she was not exactly an expert at it. It was taking her some time, and Miles finally realized that her fingers were shaking. While he was pleased to see that she was anticipating this as much as he, he didn't want her to be nervous.

He took those fingers off the fall and lifted them to his lips, kissing each one of them in turn, never taking his eyes away from hers.

There was one thing about being deaf, or as close as one could be to it — he spent a lot of time focused on the eyes and mouths of others, which meant he was well practiced at keeping someone's gaze without any qualms.

He undid his trousers himself and when he sprang free, Freddie's mouth opened and her eyes widened as she obviously gasped. Good. He grinned as he returned to his original position over top of her.

"Better?"

She nodded, tracing her fingers along his cheek.

"I want you to enjoy this, Freddie," he said, his mouth coming behind her ear once more, but this time, he nibbled the delicate lobe slightly and she leaned her head into his hand with a soft moan.

Her breath brushed against his ear and he guessed she was saying something, but he said nothing, not wanting to break this current of emotion that was simmering between them.

Instead, he took her breasts in his hands, brushing his thumbs over the nipples as she arched into him.

She was petite, yet strong, and Miles reveled in all that she had to offer. The fact that he had been keeping himself from her for weeks seemed ridiculous. All of that time when he could have been with her like this, wasted.

Well, he would more than make up for it.

He trailed his fingers from her breasts, down her side to her hips, which he cupped for a moment before continuing down to the very center of her. He stroked her once, twice, and she braced her hands on his hips and drew him toward her.

He didn't need much encouragement. He found her entrance before slowly moving into her, filling her, stretching her, and she urged him on with her hands on his back. Finally, he was fully sheathed inside her and Miles thought he would lose himself immediately from sheer plea-sure. He took a couple of deep breaths, but when she began to move he couldn't help himself from doing the same.

Soon they were rocking together as one, as though they had both been made to fit together like this, and nothing could ever keep them apart.

Miles reached down to urge Freddie on, and soon she was coming apart around him, waves of pleasure squeezing him, making it impossible for him to keep from coming himself along with her.

When the ebbs of sweet pleasure finally faded, Miles rolled to his side, his arm coming around Freddie as he pulled her in toward him, her back to his stomach. He pulled her in tightly before stroking her hair back away from her face as she nestled into him.

Never in his life had his heart been so full as in this moment.

"Freddie," he whispered in her ear, "that was…"

She turned around to face him, likely so that he could see her lips, and he loved her for it. He loved her. The thought filled him, blooming from his heart and blossoming out through his limbs. He opened his mouth to tell her, but the words didn't come. He was partly afraid that she might not say the same, which would be rejection in itself. But how could she love him, after he had kept secrets from her, had subjected her to his father as he had?

"Amazing," she finished for him, and he nodded with a smile. "You're not going to make me wait a week until we do that again, are you?" she asked, her face so serious that he could only laugh.

"No," he said, shaking his head, "most assuredly not."

Then he leaned in and kissed her once more, a kiss of promise, that from now on they would live as true as husband and wife could be.

Nothing could keep them apart. Nothing.

* * *

FREDDIE HUMMED a tune a few days later as she sat down at the breakfast table.

She hadn't known how wonderful it could be waking up in her husband's arms. Since that first night, they had spent each night together, discovering one another and all of the pleasures that could exist between the two of them.

It was all she had been longing for, and she never wanted to go back to the way things were before. She had nearly told Miles she loved him. But she had already been vulnerable enough, asking him to make love to her. She could hardly be the one to share her feelings with him first once more, or he might think her rather desperate. So instead she had shown him with her actions all that she had felt within her. Whether or not he could sense the depth of her emotion, she had no idea. But they had all the time in the world to continue to do so.

"Miles," she said carefully, not wanting to upset him, though she was very much hoping for his agreement, "we have received an invitation for dinner with Rebecca and the Duke of Wyndham. Would you care to attend?"

Their night together had been a step forward for the two of them, of that she was certain. What Freddie didn't know was whether opening himself up to her made any difference in how he might feel about spending more time in the company of others.

He looked up, eyeing her knowingly.

"You would truly like to go, wouldn't you?"

"Well," she said, placing her fork down as she crossed her hands over one another in her lap. "You are right. I would. I have always been rather used to spending time at one party or another. But I know that you do not enjoy being around people as much as I do and I understand why. If you would prefer not to go, then I will tell Rebecca that I will see her the next time we get together."

A frown crossed Miles' face. "Who all will be in attendance at this dinner?"

"Jemima, of course, and Celeste. I believe Rebecca said Lord Essex may attend. She needs one more for even numbers, but she suggested that your brother could be invited if that would be agreeable with you."

"You and your friends have discussed this already, then."

"What do you mean?" Freddie said, attempting nonchalance but knew she was failing miserably.

"The suggestion of inviting my brother — you have been thinking of ways to make me feel more comfortable. I am not sure if I like the thought of you discussing such a thing with others."

"Not at all!" Freddie said, holding up her hands in defense. "Rebecca simply said she needed another, and it was I who thought that might be helpful." She leaned toward him meaningfully. "Miles, I would never discuss anything about you that you weren't aware of — not even with the closest of my friends."

He softened. "Thank you, Freddie," he said, looking to the side as he seemed to be deep in thought. "If it means that much to you, we will go."

"Truly?" she said with great pleasure, and he nodded. "Thank you, Miles!" she said, coming around behind him to place her arms around his neck and kissing his cheek, gratefulness in her heart. "Thank you very much."

CHAPTER 17

*M*iles surveyed the table of people before him, wondering at the intelligence of his decision to attend this evening.

In front of him was the Duke of Wyndham, the man who was supposed to have married Freddie. Then there was Lord Essex, with whom she had been having such an agreeable time on the dance floor the other night. Then finally, there was his brother, ever the charmer.

Could there be a trio of men who would pose more of a threat than these?

Miles had greatly considered the option of telling Freddie no, they could not attend this dinner. But he had seen the look in her eyes when she had asked him, had understood just how much it meant to her to attend, and he didn't have it within him to say no.

So here they were.

Everyone had been quite welcoming, that much he could say. The problem was, like at all dinner parties, he was having a terrible time paying attention to the conversation. He could hear the slight din of chatter around him, but with so many different voices from all directions, it was difficult to know who was talking and when. Freddie sat beside him and attempted to notify him when someone was talking by placing her hand on his knee and joining in herself, but at times she would become immersed in her own conversation and forget to pay attention.

As the only other person at the table who knew of his difficulty, his brother, sitting across from him, had some pity for Miles and would try to signal him with a nod or a look to the side, but he wasn't always particularly attentive.

As always, Miles knew he was likely coming across as rude while those around him figured he was ignoring them. But what could he do?

"Did you know, Celeste," Freddie was looking between him and her friend now, who sat on the other side of Miles, "that Miles is the most wonderful painter? I had no idea until we were married."

Heat rushed into Miles' cheeks. "Now, Freddie, that is nothing to speak about—" Sharp pain assaulted his shin.

"You showed her your paintings?" Benjamin chimed in from across the table, having kicked Miles underneath to capture his attention. "You never show anyone your paintings."

"Well, that's because—"

"He's quite talented," Benjamin continued to the lot of them, who were now all paying attention, much to Miles' discomfort. "He can paint a portrait of great likeness, as well as some interesting landscapes. What did you think, Lady Gilmore?"

"Oh, it's Freddie, please," Freddie said, her eyes wide and bright, and Miles couldn't help the turn of jealousy at the smile on her face just for his brother. "I thought they were magnificent. I could scarcely believe Miles was the painter. I plan to hang his paintings all over the house... as soon as I can find them."

"That's really unnecessary—" Miles attempted once more, but he had lost any semblance of control of this conversation.

"My mother hung one in the dining room once," Benjamin mused. "Can't remember what happened to it, though."

Miles knew what had happened to it. His father had come in and smashed it over his knee once he knew that his son had painted it. "A pastime for ladies!" he remembered his father screaming at his mother before throwing it at a passing servant who was attempting to escape his wrath. It was the last time his mother attempted to hang one of his paintings, though she secretly praised him and had always asked to see more. When Miles left home, he had taken all of his paintings with him, though he had left his mother a few miniatures she could keep for herself.

"It's just a hobby," he said, waving a hand in the air, knowing that he sounded like Freddie now.

"Here's the thing, Lord Gilmore," Miss St. Vincent, the Duke's sister, said, leaning forward to join the conversation, "we all have hobbies, as you call them. When a hobby is a passion, however, it is more than a hobby. It's part of your purpose, part of who you are."

"Have you a *passion*, Miss St. Vincent?" Benjamin said, suddenly looking rather interested as he placed special emphasis on his words.

"I have," she said carefully, though she didn't reveal anything yet.

"What would it be?" Benjamin asked. "Music? Perhaps a bit of painting yourself? Embroidery?"

Miss St. Vincent tilted her head back ever so slightly and

laughed. Poor Benjamin looked rather bewildered, unsure of what to make of her reaction.

"My pursuits are much different, of that I can assure you," she said.

"Oh?"

"I enjoy science, Lord Benjamin," she said, her eyes lighting up. "Chemistry, actually." A footman appeared at her shoulder to refill her drink. "Brandy, please," she said before returning her focus to the table.

"Chemistry?" Benjamin repeated, bemusement within the word.

"Yes," she said with a nod. "Working with chemicals, different compounds, determining what various mixtures will result in."

"I... see."

Miss St. Vincent picked up the brandy and drank it as easily as Miles ever could have. Impressive.

"Jemima has quite the laboratory," the Duke of Wyndham said, obviously proud of his sister. "Rebecca designed it within our conservatory."

"I see," Benjamin said again, though he clearly didn't.

Perhaps Freddie had been right about inviting his brother to this gathering. Miles had not had this much entertainment or amusement in some time. He loved Benjamin, but his brother was everything a proper English lord ought to be. Everything Miles wasn't.

But this group of rather eclectic people — fellow members of the *ton* who didn't exactly fit in —made him feel more welcome than he had in some time. He looked over at Freddie, who seemed to understand his thoughts as she winked and tipped her glass toward him.

He repeated the gesture, but then Freddie was gesturing with her chin to look beyond his shoulder, and he turned to find Miss Keswick regarding him with some expectation on her face. He must have missed something.

"My apologies, Miss Keswick, could you please repeat that?"

"Of course," she said, her smile dropping slightly. "Forgive me, I should have waited until you had finished your conversation with Freddie."

"It's not that, Miss Keswick," he said quietly, for her face had flushed slightly and he knew she had thought him to be ignoring her, or, at the very least, putting her off. His own impediment was causing her to question herself. "It's just..." he took a deep breath as she looked at him with interest, and Miles sensed Freddie go still beside him, "it's that I cannot hear."

"It is rather loud in here," she said with an understanding smile. Freddie placed a hand on his knee and he gripped it within one of his.

"No," he said, shaking his head, and he could feel the attention of most of the rest of the table as his solemn expression must have alerted them to the fact that he was about to say something of significance. "I physically cannot hear. I am deaf — well, nearly deaf at least."

Freddie squeezed his hand, and when he turned to look at her, her eyes glistened with unshed tears while her lips curled up in a slight smile of support.

"Oh, Lord Gilmore," Miss Keswick said, her mouth a round O, when he returned his attention to her. "I had no idea."

"Nor I," the Duke of Wyndham said, his gaze interested. "You do an admirable job of keeping your affliction concealed."

Miles gave a curt nod, before catching his brother's gaze. Benjamin was looking at him with questionable horror. Miles could only imagine what he was thinking.

"If you could please keep this to yourselves," he asked quietly, and all at the table nodded — even Lord Essex, a man Miles hardly knew. This may have been a huge mistake. His secret might be out by the morrow. But, he realized with some shock, he didn't particularly care. So the world knew that he was deaf. What difference did it make? He was the same man. He could still function the same as he always had. Besides that, he would one day be a marquess, and a man inherited his title whether or not he could hear anything.

"Of course," the Duchess of Wyndham said with a warm smile. "Thank you for trusting us, Lord Gilmore."

He nodded at her, and then soon enough conversation resumed as though nothing was amiss.

It wasn't until afterward, when the ladies had retired to the drawing room, that his brother took him aside for a word.

"Miles," Benjamin said, his eyes wide and his hands on his hips as he spoke out of the corner of his mouth, making it rather difficult for Miles to completely understand him, "what were you thinking?"

Miles shrugged. "I've kept this secret long enough."

"Yes, but..." Benjamin ran a hand through his hair. "Couldn't you have waited a little longer? Father will be livid."

"*Father* doesn't need to know." Miles fixed Benjamin with a cautionary stare. "Do you understand, Benjamin?"

"I am certainly not going to tell him," Benjamin said as he lit a cheroot distractedly. "I love you too much. But you hardly know these people, Miles. You cannot tell me that you implicitly trust them? It's bound to get out somehow."

"Maybe," Miles said with a shrug, "maybe not. We shall see."

Benjamin was still shaking his head, clearly rattled.

"Miles… you must be careful. Father has been talking quite a bit about you lately."

"That's interesting," Miles said sardonically, "for I thought I was one of his least favorite topics of conversation."

"This isn't funny, Miles," Benjamin said, taking a swift inhale of his cheroot. "Since you married, he's been discussing whether or not you'll have an heir. How to keep you from taking an active role in overseeing your duties one day as the marquess."

"If I am the marquess," Miles said dryly, "then that means there is no worry any longer of what Father thinks."

"He has a will, though," Benjamin said with a shrug, "consider that."

"He cannot will away the title to another."

"I know that," Benjamin said quietly. "Just… be careful, Miles, all right?"

"I will," Miles said, clapping a hand on his brother's shoulder. "Thank you, Benjamin. And thank you for coming tonight."

Benjamin nodded. "They're an interesting lot, aren't they?"

"They are," Miles said with a laugh. "And somehow, I fit right in."

* * *

FREDDIE COULD HARDLY BELIEVE how much had changed in just a couple of weeks. She and Miles had begun with a marriage that had been convenient for both of them, and now… now there was emotion underlying it that was difficult to ignore. Rather than living the life she had thought she had wanted to live, she and Miles were living *together*. The times that he wasn't with her were times in which she was missing him and looking forward to their return to one another.

It was strange and yet… amazing.

"Freddie," Miles said as he came around to escort her from the breakfast table a few days following their dinner at Rebecca's house, where he had shocked her to no end, "are you planning to stay in today?"

"I am," she said, looking up at him expectantly, surprised at the pained look that had overcome his face.

"My father sent a missive this morning insisting that he is coming to call. I would refuse him, but he has written that he would like to discuss me managing another of his estates, which is something that I must accept."

"Of course you should," she agreed, although the thought of his father invading their lives once again filled her with dread.

"Perhaps it is best if you stay out of his sight," Miles suggested, relieving Freddie, although she felt a coward for leaving him to his father alone. "If he sees you, he will only use us against one another and I wouldn't like to put you through that once more."

"Very well," she said, "I can remain in my workroom. But if you need me, Miles—"

"I know where to find you," he said with a smile and a nod before bending to place a kiss upon her lips.

"Thank you, Freddie."

"Of course."

But as Freddie made her way down the corridor with a glance behind her at her husband and his reassuring smile, she couldn't help but feeling that despite how wonderful everything had been lately, something was about to go very, very wrong.

CHAPTER 18

reddie surveyed the pages in the book before her. The design looked so simple, but it had to be precise in order for it to work.

The problem was the size. She needed to find a way to make her instrument work as well as the original, but on a much smaller scale.

It was the first time she had ever considered how a hearing device worked, and she had to spend a considerable amount of time doing research. She had found all the books she could, had scoured the papers of others who had done similar work before her.

All of the hearing instruments that were currently used were basically large horns — most by people who were losing their hearing as they aged. She knew Miles would never use such a device. To do so would not only brand him as deaf but would likely make him feel ostracized by those who might judge him.

But, perhaps, if she could create something smaller, that was much less noticeable, it could make it much easier for him to hear. She had already created a prototype, but it wasn't functioning — it was simply a model of an idea she had. Now the true effort would begin, which would be to determine just how she could make such a thing work.

She had also been researching the use of hand signs and a manual alphabet, which had long been a common practice in many European communities for the deaf. Using gestures, full conversations could be had without a word spoken. She wasn't sure if Miles needed to learn such a thing, but perhaps it could help if his hearing ever worsened.

She was so focused on her work that she didn't hear any footsteps or knocks to announce the presence of another in the room until he spoke.

"Well, well, what do we have here?"

Her head shot up to find Lord Dorrington standing before her, a smirk on his face.

"This is my... workshop," she finished, standing tall, refusing to be shamed by her hobby.

"How interesting," he said snidely. "And what do you do in such a workshop?"

"Depends on the day," she said, having no interest in explaining anything further to him, knowing he would disdain whatever she said anyway.

Despite her efforts to stop him, he reached over and picked up her model. She attempted to take it back, but he turned, keeping it out of her reach.

"What would this be?"

Freddie looked around him, expecting Miles to come in and save her from further conversation with his father at any moment.

"Don't look for your husband," he said. "I told him I was leaving, and he believed me, fool that he is."

"He is not."

"Not what?"

"A fool."

Lord Dorrington snorted. "I thought you would have learned better by now," he said. "Are you not ashamed of him?"

"Of course not," she said indignantly, her hands in fists at her side.

"You should be," he said dryly, and she shook her head.

"Never," she returned fiercely. "It matters not whether he can hear. What matters is the man he is, something that you apparently do not understand."

"No?" he asked with raised eyebrows. "Then tell me, why have you gone to such great lengths to try to ensure he can hear once more?"

"What do you mean?"

He held up her model in his hand, making something that she had meant to be an example of her love seem petty and shallow.

"These are obviously aids to help him hear. Why would you be creating such a thing if not to make him more normal? Less flawed?"

"That is not my intent!" she protested. "I am doing it to *help* him."

"Are you?" he asked, tilting his head as he chuckled lowly under his breath. "That, I do not believe."

"You should."

"Well, either way, it matters not," he said, then smiled at her, a grin so wicked that it caused her stomach to roil.

He held up the model. "You will cease this. Do you know how embarrassing it would be if he wore these in public?"

A look of distaste filled his face as he brought one hand to each side of the model before he smiled at her, and then snapped it in half.

She gasped.

"How could you?"

"I am the Marquess of Dorrington. I can do whatever I wish."

"Not in our home," she said, willing her tears away. She did not want to give him the satisfaction of knowing he had any effect on her, but the frustration building within her threatened to emerge.

"And just what," he said, leaning his hands on the table so that his face was level with hers, his dark eyebrows raising over eyes that were as green as Miles', but infinitely darker in ways that had nothing to do with their color, "do you propose to do about it now?"

"I— I—" Freddie stuttered, hating herself for it, but unable to think of any witty response. For he was right. There was nothing she could do.

He began to stride along the side of her worktable, inspecting everything within.

"How very sweet," he said sarcastically. "All of the books that might help your husband."

He picked one up, read the title, and then dropped it on the floor, before following through with the rest while Freddie curled her fingers into fists at her side.

"There is no help for him," he continued as he trailed a finger along her table, before coming to the far end, where she had a wide variety of candles as test subjects set up along with her candleholder. "Keep him out of society. Do not let his secret be known to any others. That is how you help him, *Lady* Gilmore. Now, what have we here?"

"Nothing," Freddie ground out. "Candles."

"An odd thing to collect," he said, eyeing them as though he knew there was more to them. "This is a curious candlestick."

"It's nothing," she repeated, attempting nonchalance, but then, Freddie had never been much of an actress.

"I've heard of your little hobbies," he said, his words

coming out on a sneer. "Another thing best kept to yourself. The Luxington name hardly needs another risk to be sullied any further. Do you know…" He paused, picking up the candlestick and examining it, "that the Luxington family is one of the few without a stain on its reputation? We are pure, unsullied," he said, eyeing her as though she had marred the family in some way. "And I intend to keep the family line that way."

"In that you are wrong," she said, her heart beating fast as she knew her words were dangerous, that she was flirting with disaster. "For you, Lord Dorrington, are the stain upon your family. I have heard that you gamble, drink, take all manner of women. You have evil in your heart the likes of which I have never seen before. Your son is one of the best men I have ever known and yet you treat him as though he is lesser when, in fact, he is already more than you will ever be."

The marquess' face turned red as she spoke, nearing purple in color as he towered above Freddie. She knew he was attempting to intimidate her, and it was working, though she did all she could to retain a brave façade.

He took one end of the candlestick in each of hands, then raised it and brought it down, smashing it over his knee. He then reached out an arm and swept it over the table, sending all of Freddie's books, tools, and instruments flying about the room.

She leaped back with a yelp so as not to be hit by any flying object, and when the marquess sent one of the tables crashing backward, Miles came running into the room. Whether even he had heard the destruction or one of the servants had alerted him, Freddie didn't know, but relief swept over her at his presence.

"Miles!" she exclaimed, and his father turned, anger distorting his features.

"Do you think your *husband* is going to do anything for

you?" he asked, his laugh nearly sinister. "Miles has cowered from me for years!"

His back was to Miles and Freddie only hoped that her husband hadn't heard his words.

"What is the meaning of this?" Miles said, his quiet yet stern voice in such contrast to his father's harsh yell. "Father, what have you done?"

"I've destroyed the evidence of your wife's ridiculous hobby," he said with a snort. "Now, perhaps we can pass off your painting as hers — a hobby much more suited to a woman than any man at all, but especially a future marquess!"

"Miles' paintings are magnificent," Freddie said as Miles came up next to her, the two of them posing as a united front against his father.

"Magnificent," he scoffed. "Hardly."

"What you have done here today," Miles said, looking around him, his voice tightly controlled as he held his obvious anger in check, "is disgraceful. You should be ashamed of yourself."

"It is *you* who should feel shame, every day of your life," his father said, shaking a finger at them, to which Miles stepped in front of.

"Well, it was you who sired me, so anything wrong with me is much more your own fault than mine."

His father shook with fury, but before he could say a word, Miles pointed to the door.

"Get out."

"I will leave when I am ready."

Miles kept his finger pointed. "The title may be yours, the estates may be yours, Dorrington House may be yours. But this house is mine, and you will leave this instant."

His father walked forward until they were nearly nose to nose.

"But from where does your money come, Miles? Oh yes, from your family." He took a step backward, black humor now filling his eyes. "I will go, Miles, but you will rue this day. The Marquess of Dorrington does not take orders from his deaf lunatic of a son."

"I do not care what you do as long as it is not here," Miles said, his jaw clenched. "Stay out of my life, Father."

"Keep yourself out of society, and we do not have an issue," Lord Dorrington said, making for the door, before stopping, turning around on his heel. "Oh, and one more thing for the pair of you to consider."

Neither of them bothered to respond to him.

"Do all you can to prevent an heir. I will not have another imbecile in the family."

The moment he was gone, Freddie sagged into Miles' arms, grateful that, amid the chaos that surrounded them, he was the anchor she needed.

CHAPTER 19

$\mathcal{M}$iles had never been particularly prone to violence.

But if anything could have provoked him to turn to it, it would have been the scene that had just unfolded in front of him.

He had been nearly blinded with rage when he'd walked into Freddie's workroom to find his father in the throes of its destruction. His father could have torn apart anything — nearly anything — in Miles' life, but to do something that would so hurt Freddie was indescribably despicable.

Freddie had done nothing wrong besides marry him.

In all of his consideration as to where marriage could lead them — the positives and the negatives — he had thought that, as long as he could keep her from too many interactions with his father, all would be fine.

He had been wrong.

Miles stood now, his arms wrapped around her protectively, only wishing that he could have done more, that he could *do* more, to keep her from ever being vulnerable again, whether it be before his father or another. He knew he couldn't protect her from everything — she was her own woman, and would face adversity in her life as much as he would — but if only he could try.

She wasn't crying, but Miles could feel the frustration and sadness seeping from her into his own soul. She finally lifted her head to speak to him.

"How could he do such a thing?" she asked, despair on her face. "My entire workroom — destroyed."

"Had you figured out the answer to your candlestick?" he asked, and she nodded.

"I think so. Hopefully, I remember enough that I can rebuild it."

He nodded, looking around him regretfully. "I'm so sorry, Freddie," he said. "I'll have it all put back together for tomorrow."

He bent to pick up one of the books strewn about the floor, but she stopped him, taking his hand in hers.

"Don't," she said, shaking her head. "It's not just you that he has an issue with, Miles. He is embarrassed about my work. If we put it back, he will only try to destroy it again."

"I will not let him," Miles said fiercely, but she bestowed a watery smile upon him.

"Let it go, for today at least," she said, before tilting her head up, looking at him through her long brown lashes. "Please?"

Her pleading look caused a wry laugh to course through him.

"You would use your most endearing look on me at this moment."

She smiled in return. "I would."

"Very well," he sighed. "You are difficult to say no to. I will leave it — for now. But if he ever tries anything like this again, I will do all I can to ruin him."

"Miles," she said, after tugging at his sleeve. "He couldn't actually do anything to hurt us — could he?"

Miles frowned. He had no doubt that the marquess could find a way to hurt them if he was really and truly determined to do so, but he didn't want to worry Freddie any further.

"Not really," he said, squeezing her arm. "Now come," he said. "Let's go for a ride away from here and into some fresh air."

She nodded, turning to place her hands upon his arms as she looked up at him pleadingly.

"It will be all right, Miles," she said with a smile he could tell was her attempt to be reassuring — for herself as much as him. "As long as we're together."

He nodded, kissing her ever so gently on the lips. "As long as we are together."

* * *

AFTER FREDDIE FELL ASLEEP that night, Miles slipped out of bed and went to his study. He had work to do. Freddie may not feel that her work was anything worth protecting, but he had seen the look on her face when his father had nearly destroyed her workshop. This meant something to her — something more than the hobby she claimed it to be. In his opinion, she should be proud of what she was doing. She had a mind unlike most — one that could solve puzzles, fix any problem that came her way. She was incredibly unique in all of the right ways.

And he wanted others to know just how smart she was.

Miles began writing the necessary letters for the patents. If Freddie wasn't going to follow through, then he would do it for her. He just had to keep this all from his father before the despicable man ruined everything for his wife.

There was another reason Miles wanted to make sure she

was protected — one he didn't want to fathom, but that he had to consider.

For all of Miles' life, his father had taunted him with one threat after another. Sometimes he told him he would lock him away far from society, where no one would discover his secret. Other times he threatened to have him committed. Then there were the times, even when Miles was just a boy, when he told him it would have been better that he had not been born, that Benjamin was the heir.

Some days Miles wondered to what lengths his father would go to make it all come true.

If something happened to him, he had to make sure that Freddie was protected, that she would, at least, have some means of support. He knew, thank goodness, that her own family would look after her, but he'd like to know that she was able to live off of her own means as well. His paintings likely wouldn't come to much. There was an entire stack of them stored away somewhere in this townhouse — where, he wasn't entirely sure as his butler had overseen much of the move — but they could likely fetch enough for Freddie to get by for a time.

After that... well, hopefully it wouldn't come to that, but maybe her own work could earn her some income. He sighed, running a hand through his hair before rising and returning to his chambers. He sat by the glow of the fire, his gaze resting upon his sleeping wife for a moment or two before he took up his paintbrush and let his fingers work freely.

Sometimes he enjoyed doing portraits, watercolors and the like. Other times he painted more abstractly. What began as landscapes or still lifes often took a mind of their own, and by the time he was done they didn't resemble anything that anyone but he could identify.

He knew these paintings would never sell, would never

come to anything. No one wanted canvases full of random color on their wall.

But it was how his mind worked and helped him make sense of the world around him. They were his own.

He looked over at Freddie, her chocolate curls strewn about the pillow, her body entangled in the sheets where they had made love not long ago. She gave a jolt and he guessed she must have snored again, causing him to chuckle.

He didn't know how he had gotten so lucky, but he vowed to not take one moment with her for granted.

* * *

FREDDIE ROSE the next morning to a strange smell in the air of Miles' bedchamber. She turned to find him still slumbering beside her, and she wondered at what time he had returned to bed. She had sensed him leave her at some point during the night, but she hadn't said anything, not wanting to disturb him.

She left the bed now, attempting to identify the source of the smell. Ah, here by the window. It must be his paint. Unable to help herself, Freddie rounded the easel, wondering if he had painted her again, or something they could hang upon the wall. She furrowed her brow as she stared in front of her.

It was nothing, yet it was also… everything.

She nearly jumped when she felt hands upon her shoulders, and Freddie turned to find Miles behind her. How long had she stood there immobile, simply staring at the picture in front of her?

"Don't tell me you like it," Miles said with a low chuckle. "It's perfectly fine if you don't. Art is subjective."

"That may be so," Freddie agreed, "but I cannot say that I do *not* like it. It's making me think, is all."

"About what?"

"About what it is, how it makes me feel," she said. "It reminds me of... a storm cloud, I suppose. Of the whirl of emotions that come when something is unsure or unsteady." She looked up at him in realization. "Like your father."

"I paint my emotions, you could say," he said with a shrug. "Most do not understand." His eyes seemed to glow as they looked at her. "I appreciate that you do."

"I am certainly no art critic," she said with a laugh. "I usually see the more practical side of life. But in this, it simply makes sense." She looked up at him. "I'd like to see your other paintings."

"First we would have to find them," he said. "I do wonder where they could be. But there is something else that I decided last night while painting."

"Oh?"

He took a breath. "I am going to take up my seat in the House of Lords."

She clapped her hands together twice.

"Oh, wonderful, Miles!" she said with pleasure. If Miles was willing to take his seat, it meant that he not only was prepared to stand up to his father, but he was not as worried as he had been that he would be rejected. "That will be simply splendid, I am sure."

"We shall see about that," he said with a shrug. "It could be a terrible idea. But I suppose I will not know until I try."

"I'm proud of you," she said, her heart filling. "You are standing up to your father in the best way possible — by showing him what you are capable of, that nothing will hold you back."

"Yes," he said cautiously, "though I am also throwing everything right in his face. It is difficult to know how he will react. There is a chance he could rescind the use of the title, being that I am viscount by courtesy, leaving me title-less until the day I inherit."

"Would he do that?" she asked.

He shrugged, rubbing his jaw.

"I am assuming he would never do so, for it would draw more attention and create even more scandal."

"I agree. The family name is of the utmost importance to him," she asked. "I think he is all bluster."

"I wish that was all he was," Miles said quietly. "Unfortunately he is much more. I've seen him ruin men before for crossing him even in the most innocent of ways. That being said, I cannot spend the rest of my life in hiding. I will just have to be careful."

"Of course," she said, but then let out an exclamation when he took her hand in his and pulled her toward him.

"I'm so sorry, Freddie."

"For what?"

"For all of this," he waved his hand in the air. "For bringing you into this life."

"Miles," she said with a small laugh, "I believe I was the one who asked to be brought in."

"But you couldn't have known—"

She placed a finger over his lips to stop his flow of words.

"I knew who you were. And that was all that mattered. The rest of it, we will handle."

His lips quirked.

"Sometimes I wonder if you are real, or if you are a figment of my imagination come to life," he said, "for it seems you are too good to be true."

She laughed.

"You are a charmer in your own way, Miles," she said, before lifting her hands to lay them against the side of his cheeks. "But know this." Her heart fluttered. "I love you, Miles Luxington."

He slightly jerked in surprise at her words, his eyes seemingly turning various shades of green. Freddie waited patiently for him to return the words — he must love her, didn't he, after all that he had said to her?

He stepped closer, put his hands about her waist, and kissed her hard, passionately, possessively. His lips swept over hers, and as much as she wanted to push him away, to tell him that a kiss would not solve his problems, would not say all that was between them, she couldn't help but gasp when he bit her bottom lip. He took advantage, sweeping his tongue inside as she molded her body against his.

Freddie fought a battle within herself, but finally decided to allow her frustrations to ebb away. Miles was not a man who easily voiced what he was feeling. She could sense the depth of his emotion for her — she only had to be patient. As frustrating as it was, she couldn't ask him for what he wasn't ready to give.

She had to learn to wait.

CHAPTER 20

*G*uilt ate away at Miles for the rest of the day.

He could tell how upset Freddie had been when he hadn't said the words back to her. How could he describe to her just why he had kept them within?

When she said them to him again that evening as they said goodnight, he knew he had to try.

"Freddie," he said, looking into her huge, soulful brown eyes. "You know how much I care for you."

"Care… for me?" she said, raising her eyebrows, clearly expecting more.

His love for her coursed deep through his very soul. He just didn't know how he could admit it to her. It was as though if he put it out into the world, it would become a much more vulnerable point that could hurt him in ways greater than he could have imagined.

"Yes," he said firmly, holding her small hands within his. "You know I do. It's just… I'm worried that if you feel you're in love with me, you will somehow lose your goodness. I have demons, Freddie, demons left by my past, by the uncertainty that was my childhood. If it wasn't for my mother, I wouldn't even know what love was."

She said nothing for a moment. Instead, she simply studied him.

"Do you love your mother?"

He furrowed his brow.

"Of course."

"Do you feel that she has demons?"

Miles considered the question, seeing where Freddie was going with her argument but unable to think of how to respond to make her understand.

"She is troubled at times."

"And she has to live with your father, each and every day."

Miles nodded and Freddie continued.

"Loving someone does not make you become that person, Miles," she said, shaking her head sadly. "And furthermore, I wouldn't say you have demons. You have a past that might be slightly haunting, I realize. I can hardly imagine what it must have been like growing up with your father. However," she stepped back and placed her hands on her hips, "you still have it within you to love and to be loved. I should hope you recognize that."

He nodded slowly.

"I understand what you're saying, Freddie."

"Good," she said. "Oh, and before I forget — speaking of your mother, I have promised to call upon her in two days' time if you would like to join me."

Miles was shaking his head before she even finished the sentence.

"You cannot go over there."

"It's in the middle of the day," Freddie protested. "I doubt your father will even be in residence. I promised I would accompany my mother to visit. She said your mother seemed so forlorn when she asked if I would come. Would you be less apprehensive if you came along?"

The last place Miles wanted to go was his parents' home, but he should see his mother. Besides that, Freddie was right. His father was hardly ever home in the middle of the day. If Parliament wasn't sitting, then he would be out at one of his clubs of ill repute.

"Very well," he said with a sigh. "I would be pleased to accompany you."

"Wonderful," she said with a smile before quirking an eyebrow. "Just be sure you don't get too excited."

In response, Miles picked her up and tossed her on the bed. He might not have the words to tell her that he loved her just yet, but he certainly had another way to show her.

She didn't seem to mind.

* * *

MILES SPENT most of the night painting once more. Part of it was his conscience eating away at him – the other part apprehension about visiting his family. It seemed no matter what he did, Freddie was paying for his own past.

But there was something he *could* do. He could help her make amends with her own.

He spent most of the next day out of the house, doing the one thing most gentlemen such as himself enjoyed but he had never made a habit of – visiting the clubs of which he was a member. It was not particularly challenging to find the answers he sought, which only proved his suspicions that when one demonstrated a significant lack of character, it was typically not an isolated incident.

So it was later that afternoon that he found himself in a dark study, the curtains drawn to cover the sun that other-wise would have brightened the space. He tapped his fingers against the desk in front of him, slightly chagrined as the light from the fire was not nearly enough to see as well as he would have liked. But so be it. He would have to do his best. He was here now, and there was no backing down.

"Tell me, Lord Gilmore, what can I do for you?"

Lord Lovelace sat back in his wide leather chair, an eyebrow arched as though he knew exactly what had brought Lord Gilmore here. His unspoken question was rather whether Miles really wanted to take this step and address why he was here today.

"I have no wish to waste time on pleasantries," Miles said. Nor any ability to do so, for he would probably miss half of what Lovelace said in this dim study that was likely made unwelcoming for a reason. But nevertheless… "I have come with a request."

"Oh?"

"You owe my wife something."

"Do I now?" Lovelace smirked in such a way that Miles sorely yearned to reach across the table and hit it right off of him. "I believe I gave her everything she wished for."

Miles leaned forward in his chair. He was not a man particularly prone to violence, but if there had ever been a time for it, it was now.

"You bastard," he ground out, and Lovelace laughed.

"While this is all quite entertaining, Gilmore, are you going to get to your point?"

Miles stood, placing his hands on the desk as Lovelace looked up at him with amusement dancing in his eyes.

"What you owe her, Lovelace, is an apology," he said. "You took something irreplaceable from her, something you had no right to. The very least you can do is offer her an admission of your guilt. Tell her that she had no fault in the matter, but it was you who took advantage of her loving nature and trusting spirit."

"How utterly romantic," Lovelace said, his smile widening as he stood. "But you have wasted your time, Gilmore. There is no chance I will ever do anything of the sort. So go home. Home to your wife, knowing that I was the one who had her first."

Miles knew he should ignore the man. He was well aware that Lovelace was goading him on purpose. He should use his intelligence, his cunning to fight this battle.

But instead he allowed the emotions of a man in love to take over.

And he punched Lovelace right in the nose.

The man let out a cry of surprise as he lifted his hands to his nose, from which blood now gushed over his fingertips.

"You punched me!" He stated the obvious in his shock as Miles shook out his bruised hand.

"I did," he confirmed, wondering at just how good it had felt to do so. "You fully deserved it. Now, Lovelace," he said as he removed his handkerchief from his pocket and wiped off the speckles of blood that dotted his knuckles. "I expect the apology to be written to my wife by tomorrow, with your full admission of guilt. If you do not, I will be sending around a description of your current… extracurricular activities to your wife's father – the man who continues to provide you with the funds to pay for many of those addictions, despite the fact that he believes he is, in fact, paying to keep his daughter in all of her finery."

It was Miles' turn to smile at the astonishment in Lovelace's expression as he stared at him.

"You cannot be serious."

"Very. Good day to you."

More pleased with himself that he had been in quite some time, Miles donned his hat and strode from the dark office, pleased to leave it and Lovelace behind him for good.

Or so he hoped.

CHAPTER 21

reddie couldn't help the nerves fluttering about her stomach as the carriage pulled up in front of the Dorrington House for their tea with Lady Dorrington.

Despite the fact that Miles' father would not be here today, she couldn't help that the memories of the last supper they had partaken here floated through her mind. What a terrible day it had been. But today was a new day, she told herself as she shook away the thoughts. Miles' mother, Lady Dorrington, was a lovely woman. When Freddie's mother had suggested they visit together and that Lady Dorrington had been missing news of her son, how could Freddie have said no?

She smiled at Miles, whose tight lips told her that he had similar reservations. She could only imagine how he must feel every time he came here. She had one memory. He had a lifetime full of them.

Fortunately, the only inhabitants at this hour were their mothers, who were both as welcoming as could be. Freddie proudly told them of Miles' plan to take up his seat in the House of Lords as Viscount of Gilmore.

"How exciting!" Freddie's mother said. She had just learned of Miles' deafness but hadn't seemed overly concerned about it one way or another.

"Are you really going to do it, Miles?" his mother asked, her lip quivering ever so slightly in worry. "Are you going to join the House of Lords? Your father will not be pleased."

"You know, Mother," Miles said slowly, "I have learned that Father will never be pleased with anything I do unless I am tucked away somewhere far from here where no one would even know of my existence. So I have decided that all I can do now is to embrace who I am and hope that others will accept it."

Freddie squeezed his hand as she beamed at him, turning to see that his mother shared a similar expression, although her smile was still laced with worry.

"That is wonderful to hear, Miles," she said softly. "I wish you the best of luck. They will be fortunate to have you, that is for certain."

"Perhaps," Freddie said tentatively as she took a sip of her tea, "you could push for reform of some of the laws for others who are deaf. So many of them are treated as though they have no intelligence when that is so far from the truth. You are fortunate, Miles, as you had not only your mother and tutor, but some hearing as well. Imagine being completely deaf, with no way to communicate and no one to teach you. Those people who are locked away or kept from society need someone with a voice to speak for them."

Miles placed a hand on her knee, and Freddie wondered whether it was in patronization or not.

"In due time, Freddie," he murmured. "We don't all have to fix everything, you know."

She frowned at him, hoping he would understand where she was coming from. "I was only trying to help," she murmured.

"Yes, well," he said with a shrug, "some things were meant to remain broken."

She obviously understood his metaphor, though she disagreed with his statement.

"And some things," she said pointedly, "are not broken but merely have their quirks."

He raised his eyebrows at her point, but they were quickly brought back to the current conversation by their mothers, who were eagerly discussing the potential of grand-children. Freddie's cheeks went hot, and while she could tell Miles was embarrassed himself, the slightest of grins kissed his lips as though he, too, was eager for what the future might bring.

"Well, who do we have here?"

Miles' body stiffened with such tension that Freddie knew without having to look up who had entered the room.

"Horace," his mother said, standing gracefully, though worry laced her brow. "I thought you were at your clubs today."

"I was," he said. "Now I am home, only to find my wife secretly hosting Lord Gilmore and his bride," his father said, causing Freddie's stomach to fill with dread. The man couldn't even call Miles his son. "Had I known I might not have returned at all."

"Horace!"

Miles' mother's face was aghast at her husband's words, embarrassment clearly flooding her as she looked to Lady Rothwell, who wore a horrified expression.

"It's fine, Mother," Miles said, placing his arm around Freddie's shoulders. "Good day, Father."

"Before I go," his father said loudly enough for Miles to hear, and Miles looked up at him, as much as it pained him to do so. "I must discuss with you a rumor I heard."

"Oh?"

Miles turned, and Freddie could sense his annoyance that he had to look at his father in order to know what he was saying. Somehow, it seemed to give the man too much satisfaction.

"I heard you plan to take your seat in the House of Lords."

"You heard correctly," Miles said stiffly.

"It's a terrible idea," his father said. "It will not take long for others to learn about your impairment. Do not make this family a laughingstock."

Miles breathed in deeply, and Freddie looked at him anxiously. What was he planning to say?

"You know what, Father?" he responded, standing tall, "so be it. I am deaf, yes. But I can still function as well as any man. The only one who seems to have any issue with it is you. Very well. Others might learn the truth. In fact, some of them have, for I have shared it with them already. But they didn't care. As it happens, neither do I. Now, good day to you. Thank you, Mother. Lady Rothwell. It was lovely seeing you both."

Without waiting for a response, he turned on his heel and walked out of the foyer, with Freddie hurrying to keep up. Her heart ached. She had never, in her entire life, been so proud of anyone before. Miles was accepting himself, and she could not be happier, for she loved him for exactly who he was. It was time he did the same.

"Oh, Miles, you were magnificent," she said breathlessly, but before they could leave, his father caught them as they were donning their cloaks.

"For the love of..." Miles muttered under his breath when he saw the man again, and they attempted to ignore him, but Lord Dorrington wouldn't move out of the way.

"One more thing, Miles."

"What is it?" Miles said, anger lacing his words.

"Have you enjoyed your wife's invention?"

"Which one?" Miles asked tiredly. "She has created a great many. She is quite intelligent."

"The one that she created to fix you."

"To fix me?" he looked to Freddie, his eyes wide. Her heart broke at the slight glimmer of uncertainty within them.

"Yes," his father said triumphantly. "She is creating a hearing device so that she no longer has to walk around with a husband who makes both her and himself look a fool."

"That isn't true!" Freddie exclaimed from beside him, and his father cocked his head.

"No? Then what is this?"

He held up Freddie's hearing device model — or, what was left of it, from when he had broken it in half. Her anger blossomed. She had looked everywhere for it. Now to find that he had taken it, to use to grow doubt between her and Miles… she could hardly contain her anger.

"I came upon your wife creating this for you. Not to worry, Miles, I destroyed it. No son of mine will ever wear anything so… despicable."

Freddie had no idea what Miles' thoughts were as he reached out to take the model from his father.

"I see," he said, closing his fingers around the two pieces, his face expressionless. "Good day, Father."

"Good day, Miles!" his father said almost gleefully.

Miles remained silent until they entered the carriage.

"Miles," Freddie said cautiously. "Your father is wrong. I was not trying to 'fix' you. I was only trying to help."

"By helping me hear. By fixing my impairment."

"By giving you an option, if you so choose to use it," she insisted, silently imploring him to understand. "You don't need fixing."

"But you wanted to try anyway."

"Miles, that isn't it, as you well know—"

He held up a hand. "I understand, Freddie."

"No, you quite obviously do not."

"I can see how being with me would become something of a burden."

"You're being ridiculous," she said, annoyed now that he would believe his father and would think so lowly of her. "You know me, Miles," she said, leaning toward him to place her hands on his knees and force him to look up at her. "I *love* you. I love you the way you are. I was only fiddling around, trying to make something work for you. You have to understand that."

He nodded jerkily. "Of course."

"Don't sound so thrilled about it," she said, sitting back and crossing her arms over her chest, not bothering to cover her ire now. "At least I feel something for you."

He dropped his arms in exasperation.

"Don't go on about that now, Freddie," he said. "You knew when we married that you might never hear the words from me. I care for you. I enjoy spending time with you. What more do you want?"

"I want *you*," she said firmly. "You, without reserve, without holding yourself back from me. You, like you are when we make love. Warm, happy, at peace with yourself and with me. Trusting. Not suspicious of everyone's intentions. Not everyone is out to get you, Miles. We are not all like your father."

"Of that," he said, "I am certain. I'm sorry, Freddie, that you have been saddled with men unworthy of you. First Lord Lovelace, then me."

When they silently left the carriage and entered the house, Bartleby greeted them with a smile. "A note arrived for you, my lady," he said, holding out a tray, and Freddie took it absently, still more focused on Miles' last words. Why was he speaking about Lord Lovelace? She thought that had been long forgotten.

She turned to him but, as she did so, glanced down at the envelope in her hands, and her brow furrowed at the somewhat familiar script.

"What in the..." she muttered as she broke the seal and pulled out the parchment inside. Her eyes raced over the words – words of apology. Words that took all of the blame from her, words that were all she had wanted to hear for years now, since that dark day in the gardens.

But then her stomach lurched. Why? Why now, after all this time, from a man who would never mean any of it?

Remembering Miles' presence, she looked up to tell him about the contents of the envelope, but when she caught his eyes, she realized he already knew.

Her heart dropped.

"How could you?" she ground out, and the self-satisfied smile that had begun to form on his face instantly vanished.

"Excuse me?"

"Miles, you went to see Lord Lovelace, didn't you?"

"Err..." his lip twitched. "Did you or did you not finally just receive the apology you deserved?"

"Miles," she repeated, attempting patience, "did you go see Lord Lovelace?"

"I did," he said, clasping his hands behind his back, apparently proud of himself for his good deed. "He wronged you, Freddie, and it was the least I could do to insist that he provide you with a long overdue apology. I would have challenged him to a duel for dishonoring you, but that would only have called attention to the entire situation, which we obviously did not want."

"No," she said, not caring about the ire that laced her tone, "we wouldn't have wanted that."

"Freddie," he said, the proud façade dropping, causing her to nearly forgive any slight and allow him to think all was well.

But it wasn't, in any way.

"Freddie, why are you upset? I did this for you – to right the wrongs of your own past, after all that you have done for me."

"I am upset, Miles, because I asked you not to do anything about this. I only told you what happened so that you would understand, to explain my past to you. You going to Lord Lovelace… it does nothing. This is not a true apology. He doesn't mean a word of it. All you have done is cause greater animosity within a situation that didn't need any more of it."

He looked somewhat chastised, but he wasn't backing down.

"He deserved to know the error of his ways," Miles insisted. "He cannot be allowed to simply get away with what he did to you, do you not understand that?"

Freddie sighed, done with the whole thing. She was done with all of the anger and animosity between them. She just wanted a marriage of love and understanding – was that too much to ask for? One without continual struggles, between the two of them and so many around them who apparently wished to see them apart?

"I understand you wanting to make things right, Miles, more than anyone," she said wearily. "But it wasn't your place to do so."

"I am your husband," he said, his words clipped. "If it is not my right, then whose is it?"

"I thought it was mine," she said sadly. "But apparently not."

"I am sorry, Freddie," he said, not looking directly at her, but over her shoulder – at nothing, at everything but her.

"For what?"

"For not being the man you wanted – the man who would do whatever you said, leave you to do as you pleased. The truth is, I care about you, and therefore I want to be a part of your life."

"I never asked you not to be—" she began, but realized it was too late. He wasn't listening to her anymore. His back was to her and he was already halfway out the door.

"I'm going out for a bit," he said, stopping at the threshold to turn around to tell her.

"Where are you going?"

"Out," he said, and Freddie's heart broke a little at the fact that he wouldn't share all with her.

"Goodbye, Freddie."

"Goodbye," she whispered.

But he was gone.

CHAPTER 22

*M*iles didn't really have anywhere to go. He just needed out, to think, away from Freddie and her insistence of love, of her stubborn will to fix everything and everyone, her refusal to turn to him when she was the one who needed some rescuing.

Deep within him, he knew that she wasn't trying to make him into someone he wasn't, that she was only trying to help. Miles, however, was tired of being the man who needed others to function. For so long he had relied on his mother. She, along with a tutor, had taught him how to speak, how to function.

His father had been ready to ship him off to the country, pretend he never existed. In fact, if his mother hadn't been there, Miles was certain that he would have been placed in a home for the deaf and his entire existence would have been erased, leaving his brother the heir.

But it was the one thing his mother had put her foot down about.

So here he was.

He had thought that he and Freddie were in a good place.

She knew his secret and apparently loved him despite it. He was willing to take his rightful place in the House of Lords, to allow others to know of his deafness, and his refusal to cower from it.

He mulled it all over as he walked down one Mayfair street and then the next, through part of Hyde Park, and back round home. By the time he arrived, he had come to the conclusion that, as always, he had allowed his father to cause him to act far too irrationally, to get into his mind and cause him to take issue where there was none to be found.

He owed Freddie an apology. A big one.

When Miles opened the front door of his home, he was surprised by a flurry of activity. Servants flitted about here and there, primarily directed by his butler and his housekeeper, and — of course — Freddie. She stood there, a tiny general in a skirt, ordering them this way and that. They were all carrying... paintings, he realized, taking some out while bringing others in.

"Freddie?" he said, walking farther into the room. "What's going on?"

"Miles!" she exclaimed, whirling about. "You're back."

"Yes," he said cautiously, looking around him. "You've been busy," he observed.

"Oh, Miles," she said, placing her hands on his chest. "I wanted to tell you that I'm sorry. I never meant for you to feel that I was trying to fix anything. I only wanted to provide you something that could help you, so that you wouldn't feel you always needed someone with you."

He placed his hands over hers. "I understand. But I believe I am the one who should be contrite. I was being a fool, Freddie, to think that you would want to do anything but help me. As for Lord Lovelace... I was trying to right a wrong. You've done so much for me, that I could, in some small way, repay some of it."

"Can we not forget it all?" she said imploringly. "Move on? We have both made mistakes. We have both kept secrets. But I think we can also both agree that the time for that is over now. We need to be true partners, Miles, in all we do. We will be stronger if we are together."

"I agree," he said, stepping toward her, his heart warming at her words. He never would have thought such a partnership would be possible with a woman, that he could find someone who would accept him for all he was and all that he couldn't be. But he hadn't counted on finding Freddie.

She had another surprise in store for him.

"Miles… we found your paintings."

"I never looked very hard for them," he mused. He hadn't done so on purpose. She had liked the painting he had done of her, had said she appreciated his landscape, if it could be called such a thing, but he was worried about what she would really think of the lot of them.

"Miles, they are *magnificent*," she said, her eyes glowing. "I immediately asked the housekeeper to hang them throughout the house."

"All of them?" he asked, raising his eyebrows.

"Many of them," she responded, tilting her head. "I do not know much about art, Miles, but I know what I like, and I like your paintings. Even the strange ones."

He snorted. "The strange ones were not for anyone's eyes but my own."

"Well, they are now on the walls in the foyer and the drawing room, so I must tell you that they will soon be seen by all who enter our home."

A slight bit of unease coiled through him, but before he could pay it any mind, she slipped her arm through his and leaned in close.

"I've hung a few in our bedroom."

Our bedroom. He rather liked the sound of that.

"Would you like to go see?"

She looked up at him with her dark lashes fluttering low, and desire burned through him at her gaze.

"I would very much like to do so."

They laughed as they rushed up the stairs in nearly a race to the bedroom.

Freddie pushed open the door, twirling around with her arms in the air in front of one of his paintings that adorned the opposite wall. It was a purple and blue haze, one that showed all of the desires that had swirled up within him upon watching his wife, before it had flowed down his fingers, and through the paintbrush to the paper.

"You couldn't have picked a more perfect painting for this room," he said softly, placing his hands upon her shoulders.

"It does match the navy curtains, doesn't it?"

He chuckled. "It does. But it's more than that. It evokes all of the things that I wish to do to you."

"Oh." Her pink lips formed a perfectly round circle. "I see."

"Shall I demonstrate?"

It seemed she had lost her ability to speak, for she only nodded.

He grasped her shoulders and twirled her around so that her back was to him, before he carefully undid each button, sliding it through its eyelet. As he did so, he kissed the soft skin that was bare to him on her upper back, then let her feel the heat of his lips through the thin material of her chemise.

He slipped his hands underneath the caps of her sleeves, then slid them slowly down her shoulders, allowing his fingers to drift over her skin, teasing her with his touch. The top released, the lavender dress slid from her body to pool on the floor, and he then dispensed with the chemise so that it, too, joined it.

Miles smiled at her standing in front of him, bare to his

sight. He lifted her before placing her on the bed, parting her legs so that he could fit between them. He knelt in front of her, gazing up at her reverently.

"You're so beautiful."

Her cheeks flushed.

"I'm not, really."

"You are," he insisted. "And it is time you believed it. I wouldn't tell you that if it wasn't true. You married me without false compliments, and I'm not about to start telling you lies now. I already have you in my bed, remember?" he said with a wink, and she laughed.

"Well... thank you, Miles."

He ran his fingers down the soft, smooth skin of her waist to cup her hips, which his hands fit around just perfectly, as though they were made for him to hold. He gently urged her toward him, before lifting a hand to part her at her center and find her tender nub.

She nearly shot off the bed at his touch, but he held her grounded to it with his other hand. Freddie placed her hands around his chin, gently tilting his head up to look at her.

"You're not telling me to stop, are you?" he asked, raising an eyebrow, and one corner of her lips quirked as she shook her head.

"No," she answered, but kept his chin firmly in her hand. "But I have one request."

"Which is?"

"I'd like your shirt off while you do it."

He grinned at her then.

"That, my lady, I can agree to."

It took him nearly no time at all to bare his torso to her, and then he resumed where he had left off. She leaned back on the bed, resting on her elbows as he bent and tasted her, reveling in her response as she twisted her fingers into his hair and pulled so hard it nearly hurt, but it was pain he welcomed. He dipped one finger into her, then two, and when she exploded, she gripped him with her thighs as she pulsed around his fingers.

He climbed up her body onto the bed over top of her, and when he nudged his erection against her opening, she welcomed him with her heat and her arms, which gripped him around his back, holding him tightly as he rocked against her. It didn't take long for him to find his fulfillment, coming into her with as great a force as he could imagine.

He rolled off of her and she tilted her head to the side, looking at him with a smile on her face.

"So…" she said, "does this mean I'm forgiven?"

He laughed and hauled her against his side.

"I think I'm the one that should be asking for forgiveness for being so foolish as to think you would have any greater motivation than helping me. I suppose it is time we began to trust one another, isn't it?"

Her smile faded ever so slightly, though her lips were still curled in a slight smile as she regarded him.

"I trust you, Miles."

He nodded, holding her warm brown eyes with his.

"I appreciate that," he said, feeling the boor for being unable to return these words either. But they would be a trite lie, for he had questioned her but a short time earlier. He would work on it, though. He traced his fingers over her temple, curling a strand of her silky hair around his finger.

"You are everything to me, Freddie," he said quietly. "You know that, don't you?"

She smiled. "Isn't it funny to think, Miles, that we married for nothing more than convenience?"

"I have a confession."

"You do?" she raised her brows.

"I always had a bit of a tendre for you," he admitted, and she lifted herself up on one elbow.

"You hardly ever paid me a lick of attention when we were young!"

"I admired you from afar," he said with a bashful grin. "Every time I was close to you, it seemed my tongue tangled in my mouth and I couldn't emit any words that made any sort of sense."

"Oh, Miles," she said, pillowing her head on her hands. "If only you had told me, I wonder where we would be now?"

"Hopefully in the same place?" he suggested, and she laughed.

"Or we might have been married long ago and had a brood of children by now."

He sobered somewhat at the thought.

"I hope…"

"Yes?"

"I hope if we do have children who have a similar affliction to mine that they are able to have a full life. That we can do for them more than my mother was able to do for me."

She sat up at that, reaching a hand over to grip one of his.

"Of course we will," she said firmly, and he loved her for it. "The child will have two parents who will do everything possible to make life easier. Are you aware of sign language?"

"A bit," he said, furrowing his brow. "But it seemed easier to learn to speak and understand everyone else than learn a language that few would understand."

"Well, it's an option," she said, lifting one of her graceful shoulders. "And one we could always pursue."

"You do think of everything, don't you?" he asked with affection.

"Is that a bad thing?" she asked, and he shook his head.

"Not at all. Now come here," he said, bringing her head down to his. "I have a little more I need to share with you."

She giggled as she rolled over top of him and into the bed.

Freddie, this beautiful wife of his, was healing deep

wounds within him — wounds he never thought would mend.

Miles only hoped that one day, he could repay some of her love, returning some of that same light to her life.

It was much to strive toward, but he hoped he could find a way.

It was the least he could do.

CHAPTER 23

"It's remarkable, really," Jemima said as she sank back into the folds of the blue brocade sofa in her brother's drawing room. It had become their place of choice for their weekly meeting. Rebecca had designed the most beautiful room, that reminded them all of standing on the shore of the ocean — although Freddie had only seen the sea a few times when she was a girl.

"I never would have known had he not told us," Jemima continued. Freddie was unsure about discussing Miles' hearing condition with her friends, but he *had* told them of it himself.

"I had an idea for a hearing device," Freddie said now, slightly changing the topic of conversation.

"Oh?" Rebecca said, leaning forward, intrigued. "Tell us about it."

Freddie began to explain the cones she had devised, that would be connected by a thin wire around the back of the head. She told them of her research and what had previously been invented, but she saw she was beginning to bore them and quickly finished.

"Anyway," she said, "I still have work to do, but I believe I can get there."

"Extraordinary," Celeste said, leaning forward with her elbows on her knees, her emerald green eyes wide and open. "Is that all you are working on?"

"Well, actually…" Freddie began, at first slightly self-conscious, but then remembered that her friends were interested and understanding, unlike most women would be. Even her family didn't completely understand her. Oh, they were lovely and supportive and would smile and nod as she spoke, but Freddie could tell that behind their smiles were bemusement over why she spent her days as she did.

"Actually, I am working on something else," she said shyly, and her friends looked at her expectantly. "I've devised a candlestick that should slow the rate of burn of candles," she explained, though a slight twinge turned in her stomach when she remembered what had happened to her prototype. "It's been working, but I think I can make it even better. It will just take some tweaking."

"Fascinating," said Celeste, her voiced laced with admiration. "I wish my mind worked like yours."

"Ah, but that's the beauty of it all," Freddie said. "Yours works in ways I could never fathom. What you see in the stars… knowing how to search them, which star is where, how they interconnect… to me, it seems they've all just been thrown up in the sky to light our way."

"That might not be altogether untrue," Celeste said with a smile. "Although you're right, there is far more to it than that."

"Which is why we are fortunate there are people like you to unearth the secrets above us," Freddie said, and they shared a smile.

Their weekly gatherings left Freddie in the best of moods, and she hummed a cheery tune as she walked home from

Rebecca's London home on the outskirts of Mayfair. She had just turned up the walkway to her own townhouse when she heard shouts coming from within. Looking up to see the front door wide open, Freddie's heart began to pound and she lifted her skirts in her hands and raced into the house.

She froze when she reached the front foyer. Miles was fighting to free himself from two big brutes of men, who each had a hold of his arms, which were held behind his back. His father stood before him, a satisfied smile on his face. Another man, with a rather long beard and a burly frame, stood to the side with a smug expression as he swirled a piece of paper within his fingertips.

"You are despicable," Miles was saying, practically shaking with fury as he stared down his father. "I know you hate me, but to commit your own son—"

"I haven't looked at you as a son since you were three years old," his father said cruelly, and Freddie saw the hurt gleam in Miles' eyes and her heart broke along with his. "I should have done this years ago."

"What is the meaning of this?" Freddie asked, finally breaking into the scene before her as she looked back and forth between Miles and his father.

"Freddie," Miles said quietly, shaking his head in warning, but Freddie would not be deterred.

"Your husband," Lord Dorrington said, puffing out his chest with authority, "has gone mad."

"What?" Freddie exclaimed.

"I have here a doctor who has certified his lunacy," Lord Dorrington continued before plucking another piece of paper from his pocket. "And here is the certification from another doctor as well."

"Whom I have never even met," Miles said, his voice dripping with anger.

"It doesn't matter," his father said briskly, returning the

paper to his pocket. "With two certifications, you are now to be removed from your home."

"To where?" Freddie cried as shock coursed through her at Lord Dorrington's drastic actions and the thought that, with one vengeful act, her husband could be taken from her. And for what? For simply existing? For not being the perfect son that his father required? It couldn't be. There was no way this was legal, no possibility that Lord Dorrington could get away with something like this... was there?

"He will be taken away from London for his own safety – and yours, Lady Gilmore," Lord Dorrington continued. "I will not have him put into a place where his name could be on public record. We wouldn't want the world to know that the son of Lord Dorrington has gone mad. No, we will find another excuse for the public, something that will explain why my son has had to leave London."

"That's preposterous!" Freddie said, looking at Miles, whose steady gaze was upon her. She could read the despair in his eyes, and her own anguish grew even stronger at the realization that Miles had nearly given up. "Miles," she said desperately, willing him not to surrender, "this cannot be allowed!"

"He's been trying for years to do away with me," Miles said, his voice even and steady – how, she had no idea. "I suppose our marriage has been enough to push him over the edge."

"Your marriage should never have happened," the marquess said, beginning to pace the foyer. "I should never have allowed it. But now, I will correct it — before it's too late."

Too late, what would make it too late? Freddie wondered, before realizing that part of the issue was to ensure she didn't become pregnant with an heir. By removing Miles, his father could ensure the two of them were kept apart.

"Well," Freddie said, attempting to keep down the panic that clawed at her throat, "I will go with him, then. Just let me get my things—"

"Absolutely not," roared Lord Dorrington. "We cannot have you in the presence of a madman. I worry about you. What would your father think if I allowed you to remain with him?"

Her father. Perhaps her family could help. Freddie simply had to get word—

"Not to worry, my dear," the marquess said sarcastically. "I have already told your father everything – including the fact that I will ensure your safety."

Freddie's hopes fell. Would her father believe her over Lord Dorrington? She couldn't be sure, but the fact he had already received word did not work in her favor.

"My husband is no more mad than anyone else outside this window," Freddie protested, waving to the street in front of them. "There is no viable reason that you could—"

"No?" Lord Dorrington said, a sick smile crossing his face. "There are actually many reasons, as the good doctor here has determined. First of all, there is the fact that Lord Gilmore cannot hear. That alone is a sign of madness that many have been committed for."

The doctor nodded in agreement, despite his pained smile.

"I have, however, allowed Lord Gilmore to live within society despite that," the marquess continued, as though he had done Miles a great favor. "But now, I'm afraid, his madness has surfaced and there is nothing further that can be done."

"What are you talking about?" Freddie said, hearing the slight wail in her voice but unable to do anything about it.

"It's all around you," the marquess said, his hands splayed wide. "His madness is upon these walls. Look at these paintings. Do they seem to you the work of a sane man?"

Freddie's stomach plunged in sickness as she looked at Miles' paintings surrounding them. This was her doing. She was the one who had insisted they hang Miles' artwork, despite its unconventionality. She had been proud of him, but now... now his father was using them against him.

"They are the work of a *creative* man," she countered, but Lord Dorrington was shaking his head.

"I have stayed to argue with you for far too long," he said before laughing rather cruelly. "And really, it doesn't much matter what you think, Lady Gilmore. Your opinion doesn't make any difference. All I need is the certifications, which I have right here. You, my dear, have simply the affection of a wife for her husband. It is admirable but meaningless. No more time to waste. Let's go."

He motioned to the door, and despite Miles' attempt to fight them off, the two men holding him pulled him through it.

"No!" Freddie cried, hurrying in front of them and throwing herself at Miles. She knew it was ridiculous — she was half the size of one of the two men — but she couldn't help but try to beat them off, to free Miles from them. "You cannot take him!"

"Oh, but I can," Lord Dorrington said. "Move, woman."

"Miles!" Freddie cried desperately, and when he looked down at her, his eyes had lost their despair but were filled with something else. They glistened with unshed tears, and Freddie realized that her own were running down her cheeks.

"Don't leave me," she cried, bringing her hands to his face.

"I promise," he said softly, "that I will do all I can to come back to you."

His father snorted.

"But if I cannot," Miles continued, "then you must live, Freddie, do you understand? Live the life you were meant to. Create your inventions. Keep your heart open. Be the woman you always wanted to be. Don't lose hope. Can you do that?"

"I will not," she said fiercely. "I will have you back home with me."

"Perhaps someday," he said softly, but his eyes belied his words, conveying something different, something that haunted her to the depths of her very soul.

"Don't give up, Miles," she said, pounding her small fists upon his chest. "Please, you can't."

"Freddie, stop. Look at me," he said, his steady, even tone finally willing her to cease her movements and do as he said. "You are the best thing that has ever happened to me. Never forget that."

At that, the men tore him away from her and half-carried, half-dragged him down the walkway to the waiting carriage, while Freddie fell to her knees at the doorway as shuddering, soul-racking sobs overcame her.

She stayed there, staring after the place the carriage had disappeared, until the housekeeper came and collected her, leading her to her room.

Later that night, Freddie finally fell into an exhausted sleep.

When she woke the next day, however, despite her red-rimmed eyes and hollow soul, she was filled with something else — determination.

She was going to find her husband and bring him home to her.

No matter what it took.

CHAPTER 24

*F*reddie berated herself as she dressed. Had she been of sound mind, she would have thought immediately to have followed Miles in her own carriage. Now, she had allowed far too much time to pass, and she would have no idea where Miles might be.

However, others might know. She just had to convince them to tell her, despite what it might mean for them.

Her maid eyed her with compassion and pity as she dressed, but Freddie decided that she would not be someone all would feel sorry for.

"There's got to be a way to get him out, Louisa," she said to her maid, who nodded, through her expression told Freddie she doubted her ability to do so. "There just has to be."

While it wasn't far to Dorrington House, Freddie decided to take the carriage, for she was hopeful that she would make a discovery that would call for the need to travel.

Freddie pushed back her shoulders and held her head high as she strode confidently up the steps to the home of Miles' parents. The marquess held more power than she could ever imagine, it was true, but she refused to allow herself to be cowed by him. She could admit to herself that it was her most incessant hope that he was not home, but that was likely too good to be true. Somehow, whether he was here or not, she had to get through to Miles' family. It was the only way.

The butler looked a little sick when he answered the door to her. Apparently, word had made its way through the servants of what had occurred.

"I would like to see Lord Benjamin or Lady Dorrington, please," Freddie said, but before the butler could say another word, Lord Dorrington filled the doorway.

"I thought you might decide to pay us a visit this morning," he said as he eyed her with an evil glint. "Get out, Lady Gilmore. You are not welcome here."

"I wish to see Lady Dorrington," she said, standing as tall as she could. "To share our sorrows about what you have done to your son."

"I have but one son now," he said. "Lord Benjamin. He is not within."

"Lady Dorrington—"

"Is not receiving visitors," he said, walking toward Freddie so that she was forced to take a step back. "I am the master of this house, Lady Gilmore. No one here is going to do your bidding over mine, do you understand?"

Fury raced up from her very center, burning the back of her throat as she pointed a finger at the marquess. "I will find Miles," she promised. "I will have whatever terrible commitment you have forced upon him reversed. Just you wait and see."

The marquess laughed, only causing Freddie to seethe even more.

"Good luck, Lady Gilmore." He turned from her back to

the corridor but then stopped, holding up a finger. "One more thing."

Freddie balled her fists at her side, knowing whatever he had to say would be something she didn't want to hear.

"If you do decide to continue on this ill-fated pursuit of justice, there will be consequences. Your husband will not be the only certified lunatic in the family."

"What are you talking about?" she couldn't help but ask, her heart beating frantically in her chest.

He looked at her down his nose. "A woman who spends her days attempting to dream up all manner of useless inventions, thinking she is smart enough to do a man's work? That is enough to have you certified as well."

"You're the one who is insane," Freddie ground out, but he simply laughed again.

"Good day, Lady Gilmore!" he called out, waving farewell. "And best of luck!"

The butler gave Freddie a sympathetic smile which Freddie accepted with a nod, though it only further fueled her. She would not spend the rest of her life as the woman who servants pitied.

She had to find a way to talk to Benjamin or Lady Dorrington. But how?

When she entered her carriage and took a seat, hanging her head in her hands, she screamed in surprise when another hand brushed against hers.

"Benjamin!" she finally managed when her heart slowed. "*What* are you doing?"

"I had to talk to you, obviously, and I certainly couldn't do so in my house."

"Do you know what your father has done?" she asked, hearing the desperate raggedness of her voice. When she leaned back against the squab, however, she finally noticed that the typically easygoing, free-spirited Benjamin was visibly shaken.

"I know, Freddie," he said, running his hand through his hair in a move that was so like Miles it made her heart ache. "I don't have words for it. My father... he's never been able to accept the fact that Miles is different."

"But he isn't *mad*, Benjamin," she protested. "Surely he can't just make the decision to certify his son as a lunatic without there being an avenue to protest it."

"Unfortunately, when one is a marquess, he can pretty much do whatever he chooses," Benjamin said, a pained expression upon his face. "We can protest it, yes, but he holds far more power than you and I. Besides that, to *move* Miles from wherever he is, we would have to prove that he is being treated inhumanely. To actually overturn the certification of lunacy, we would need the doctors to attest to his sanity. They are unlikely to do so when they are under my father's pay."

"Where *is* Miles?" she asked, hope springing in her breast that Benjamin would take her there. If she could only *see* him—

"I don't know," Benjamin said, his shoulders slouching. "My father knows better than to tell me."

Freddie leaned forward, placing a hand upon his knee. "You have to find out."

"I know," Benjamin said, though doubt crossed over his face. "I shall try."

"You must do better than that," Freddie said insistently. "You can do this, Benjamin. You have to — for your brother."

Benjamin nodded slowly. "All right, Freddie. I'll do all I can."

"How is your mother?" Freddie asked gently, and Benjamin's lids dropped low over her eyes.

"Not well. She has taken to her bedchamber and refuses

to leave. Her spirits are low. I don't know what to do, Freddie, I really don't. My father—"

"Will not have the final say, Benjamin," she said firmly, her spirits and resolve rising from being the strong one for Benjamin. "If nothing else, we will find Miles and we will spirit him away from here. Perhaps to Scotland, where there will be less chance he will be pursued. As much as I do not want to see your father win, I would rather have Miles in good health and free than trapped away somewhere."

"There's something else."

Freddie's heart dropped.

"What could possibly be worse than the situation we are currently in?"

"It's just… I don't know for certain, Freddie, but from the way my father has spoken…"

Freddie did all she could to hold onto her patience, to allow Benjamin to say what was on his mind, but she could barely keep herself from leaning forward and shaking the words out of him.

"If a man is mad, he still holds the title, as we all know," Benjamin finally continued.

"Like King George."

"Yes, exactly," he said. "Someone else would simply act for him, managing the estates and the like. There is only really one way for the title to pass onto the heir."

Freddie froze. She wasn't sure if she was even still breathing once she understood what Benjamin was suggesting. The marquess wouldn't… or would he?

"Do you really think—" the words caught in her throat and Freddie cleared it as best she could "—that your father would *kill* Miles?"

"I heard him talking to the doctor," Benjamin said, his voice hoarse. "There was the suggestion that if some of the treatments went too far… he wouldn't be upset."

"We have to find him, Benjamin," Freddie said, refusing to allow her very worst fears to invade. "You must determine what your father has done with Miles, and you must do so *right now*, do you understand?"

Benjamin nodded.

"I am going to acquire some help," she said. "When I return, you best be ready with some information. We will be waiting in the carriage in the mews in an hour. I shall see you shortly."

Benjamin nodded again curtly and then Freddie was off. Lord Dorrington might be a marquess, but she could top that. She knew a duke.

"You CANNOT BE SERIOUS!" Rebecca's eyes were wide as Freddie gripped her arms, recounting the tale as quickly as she could. The duke paced back and forth across the drawing room floor, while Jemima sat on the couch in shock.

"We will help him," Jemima said, standing, "of course we will."

"We will need additional people we can trust," the duke muttered, crossing his arms over his chest. "I'm not sure if we can do anything to prove Gilmore sane, but at the very least, we can rescue him from wherever he is. We need more manpower."

"And woman-power," Jemima added, but the duke waved his sister away.

"Hopefully his brother can come through," he said. "Archie will come."

"Archie?" Freddie asked.

"My valet."

"Can you trust him?"

"I've known Archie since I was five years old. I trust him as much as any family member."

Jemima nodded in agreement

"Very well," Freddie said, grateful for any help.

"We must collect Celeste," Jemima insisted, but the duke shook his head.

"There's not enough time," he said. "Besides, she will simply hinder us. One more body to take care of."

"She's quite intelligent," Jemima defended her friend. "I'm sure she will be of help to us. She lives close. We can still be at Dorrington House by the agreed-upon hour."

"Very well," he said with a sigh. "We best get moving. We do not have a lot of time."

So it was that they found themselves moving through London a short time later, the carriage full of silent, stoic, yet determined men and women. Freddie grew slightly nervous when Benjamin didn't immediately come out of his town-house, but after a few minutes, he arrived.

He looked around at the lot of them when he joined them in the carriage, before taking the one open seat.

"He's at one of our estates. A small one, where we never visit," he said without greeting. "It's not far. It will take but a couple of hours to arrive. Are you sure you all want to come along?" he said, looking around at them each in turn. "I don't know what will be awaiting us when we get there. Perhaps the ladies best—"

"No," Freddie said forcefully. "I am coming, no matter what."

She couldn't say the words. She refused to believe that anything had happened to Miles. It couldn't have. She was sure that she would know, deep in her very bones, if — she couldn't even think it.

"We will be there to help release him, and then I will go

with him to Scotland," she said. "They couldn't force him back from there, could they?"

"I suppose if someone in Scotland wanted to remove him back to England, they could," the duke said. "But I very much doubt that anyone in Scotland would care enough to comply with an English lord's wishes."

"That's what I hoped," Freddie said, breathing deeply while Jemima took her hand.

The next two hours were the longest of Freddie's life. The entire ride, all she could think about was what was currently happening to Miles, what horrors he could possibly be enduring, what he could have withstood while she had done nothing but despair. Why had she not gone into action sooner? Why had Benjamin not done more earlier?

"I should have done more," she finally said, breaking through the tense silence, and Celeste placed a hand over hers.

"That's enough of that," she said firmly. "Looking back on what you could have done will not help your husband. Now is the time to make a plan of action, do you understand?"

Freddie nodded. "You're right, Celeste," she said. "So, what are we going to do?"

"What do *you* think we should do?" Rebecca asked.

"Well," Freddie said, breathing deeply as she collected her thoughts. "Some will depend on the layout of the estate, which is where Benjamin will come in — as well as you, Rebecca. But here is what I'm thinking."

CHAPTER 25

*H*ad this happened to him two months earlier, Miles was sure he would have given up, would have finally given in to his father's insistence on seeing him dead.

But that was before. Before falling in love. Before Freddie.

Now Miles was torn. Part of him wanted nothing more than to continue to fight, to live to spend another day — all his days — with Freddie. His soul longed to see her again, to be with her again, to have the opportunity to tell her that he loved her.

Why could he not have told her how he felt? He had known he had loved her for so long now, yet he had not been able to share the words with her. What a fool he had been. Now he might never have the opportunity, and she would spend the rest of her life not knowing how he had truly felt about her.

Another part of him, however, the rational, reasonable part that was crying out to be heard, told him that it was better this way. She was better off without him, without his family, without having to be tied to him and his madness for the rest of her life.

Not that it mattered.

Miles had already circled his sumptuous prison multiple times but could find no apparent way to escape this bedchamber which had obviously been awaiting him for some time now. The windows were locked and barred; the door seemingly locked by multiple methods. The room was bare of anything that might be used as a weapon, and Miles himself had been kept to the bed for much of his time since he had arrived, as clearly some sort of sedative had been placed in his food. He had solved that issue by refusing to eat any more, but he knew he could only continue that for so long until he would be ravenous.

He sat down now in one of the wooden chairs, resting his head in his hands. He closed his eyes and pictured not his current surroundings, with the all-white unadorned walls, the blue four-poster bed, the oak table, and matching chairs. He was grateful for once that he could hardly hear, for he was aware that the only sound in the room was likely the ticking of the mantel clock above the fireplace. In the near-silence, he had caught a hint of the sound when he had walked by it earlier that day. If he had to hear it over and over again, he knew it would likely send him into actual madness.

The door suddenly opened and in walked a mustached man in sensible attire of a simple jacket and trousers. He pushed his spectacles farther up his nose as he shut the door firmly behind him and took a chair across from Miles.

He began writing something on the notepad in front of him when Miles interrupted.

"You can speak to me, you know," he said wryly. "I'm not sure what my father told you, but I am quite capable of conversation."

The man who Miles assumed to be the doctor looked up in surprise. "But I thought you were—"

"Deaf? I am, mostly," Miles said. "But I can hear enough, especially in the silence, and if I am looking at you, I know what you are saying."

"I see," the doctor said, seemingly much less sure of himself now. "I am Doctor Brown."

"What are you going to do with me?" Miles asked. "I have no madness to treat. My hearing is not going to change. You know as well as I do that there is no need to keep me here."

The doctor flicked his pen against the table.

"Yes, well… there is also the madness the marquess has asked to cure."

"I am no more mad than you are, Doctor!" Miles protested, but the doctor continued on as if he was the one who couldn't hear.

"Tell me about the paintings," he said. "Where did the ideas for them come from?"

Miles groaned and leaned back, lacing his fingers through his hair.

"The paintings are nothing. An idle amusement. Look…" He leaned forward once more in the chair, "I am not mad, and I can tell that you are well aware of that fact. I am here because my father would like to be rid of me. Can we quit with the formalities and get on with it?"

The man shifted uncomfortably in the chair. "Here is the thing, Lord Gilmore," he said, tapping his pen on the table once more. "I am not your only physician."

"No?" Miles raised an eyebrow. "Surely, my father is not actually trying to cure me?" he asked sarcastically.

"I cannot say for sure," the doctor shook his head. "But my colleague, Doctor Gibbons — the physician who brought you here — uses methods that are far more… aggressive than mine."

"Like?"

"Bleeding. Cupping. Hydrotherapy."

Miles' heart began to beat slightly faster.

"When is this therapy set to begin?"

"Today, my lord," the doctor said, looking away from him, discomfort on his face. "I do urge you to eat. You will need your strength."

"I am not taking your drugs." Miles crossed his arms over his chest. "I would rather be in control of all of my faculties."

"Perhaps," the doctor said cryptically, "perhaps not."

Miles wasn't entirely pleased with the sound of that, but the doctor looked down at him with some sympathy before taking his leave.

"I suggest, Lord Gilmore, that you cooperate as best you can," he said with a sigh. "It will be much easier."

He then opened the door, but when he did, another figure rushed through the door and into the room.

"Miles!"

"Freddie?" Miles stood up in shock." What are you doing here?"

"Oh, Miles, I had to see you!" She rushed at him, throwing herself in his arms. All Miles could do was hold on tightly.

"How did you find me?"

"Benjamin," she explained.

"How did you gain entrance?"

"The butler. He was quite kind and understanding," she said, then leaned in as close as she could. She whispered something in his ear, but he had no idea what she said. Brown was still standing at the door, his expression rather uneasy for he was clearly unsure of whether he should take Freddie from the room or allow their reunion to continue. Freddie stole a glance over her shoulder and, seeing him, took a deliberate step back from Miles instead.

When she saw that she had his attention, she began to mouth the words.

"We must escape," she said, to which he attempted to stealthily nod his head. "I have plans," she continued. "We will go to Scotland. Now we just have to get you out of here."

"Doctor Brown?" Miles looked to the door. "Can I have a moment with my wife, please?"

"I'm not sure…"

"Please, just a moment? There is nowhere we can go, and we promise to be on our best behavior."

The doctor looked down the corridor one way and then the next before nodding curtly.

"Very well. But just a minute."

"Thank you."

Miles took a few precious seconds to gather Freddie in his arms and hold her as close and as tightly to him as was humanly possible before setting her back on her feet.

"I can still hardly believe that you are here," he murmured. "Though I welcome your presence all the same. I am glad to see you again, Freddie, even if it is just this one last time."

"Don't be ridiculous," she said, swatting him. "We will get you out of here, and we will leave England."

Miles shook his head as his heart weighed heavily in his chest.

"I cannot make you do that, Freddie."

"No one is making me do anything."

"All right, then. I will not let you do that."

"I will do as I please," Freddie said, narrowing her eyes at him. "And I am going to get you out of here."

Miles took her hands in his. "I have already ruined your life enough as it is," he pleaded with her. "Do not allow me to do so even more. From now on, no matter what, you are going to be branded the wife of a madman."

"I don't care!"

"Yes, you do. Or you should. Freddie, your life is here, with your friends, with your work. I cannot ask you to give all of that up to live in Scotland."

"I will make new friends," she said stubbornly. "All that matters is that I have you."

"It's not that simple," Miles persisted. "You might not have me forever. All I want is for you to live your own life, create your inventions, and find a man who can give you the life you deserve to live."

"But that's just it," Freddie said, stepping up and running her hands over his cheeks. "The only life I want now is one with you. No other life is worth living. What is it going to take for you to understand that?"

The door burst open once more, leaving Miles to question his earlier wonder that he might die of boredom, for it would be impossible with all of these comings and goings.

"No visitors!" the man in the doorway bellowed. In walked the doctor who had been with his father in London, who had signed the final certification of lunacy and come to collect him.

Dread filled Miles upon his return.

"Lady Gilmore," Dr. Gibbons said now, his bulky, commanding frame filling the doorway. "You must leave at once."

"I will not," Freddie said, standing in front of her husband as though she could be enough protection to keep all away from him.

The two burly men from earlier suddenly bookended the doctor.

"If you do not leave, then you will be forcibly removed," the doctor said.

"You wouldn't lay your hands on a viscountess," Miles said firmly, but the doctor shrugged nonchalantly.

"I am in the pay of a marquess, who I am sure would not care what I do."

Of that, Miles was sure.

"It's all right, Freddie," he said gently in her ear. "Go."

"I will not," she repeated, but she turned around to face Miles this time. Tears swam in her eyes, and Miles wondered what he had done to deserve the love of such a woman.

"Go home, Freddie," he said again, wrapping his hands around her shoulders. He no longer wanted her to see him like this. He would prefer she stay far, far away — from him, from his father, from this entire sordid situation.

He leaned in close to whisper one final warning in her ear.

"If you find that you are with child," he said in what he hoped was a low enough voice that no one else could hear, "then you must hide. If you have a son, you must take him away from London or anywhere my father might discover you until after my father's death. Do you understand?"

He leaned back to look into her eyes, and she nodded, though her tears began to fall now.

"Go."

He put a hand on her back to help her to the door.

When she nearly got there, he leaned in and whispered, "I love you."

She only had time to turn around and look at him with as much desperation as he felt before the door shut behind her.

CHAPTER 26

"We have to get him out," Freddie said desperately now to the collection of men and women standing in front of her. "We just have to. Lord only knows what that doctor is doing to him, even now. He is evil and he is working for evil — I'm sorry, Benjamin, but it is the truth — and the way Miles was talking... I don't think he believes he is ever going to get out of that house alive."

Benjamin rubbed a hand over his face as he paced along what had already become a worn path in the brush just beyond the estate.

"Don't talk like that," Celeste said firmly, taking Freddie by the elbow. "We will get him out, Freddie, I promise."

"But how?"

The duke was looking up at the manor.

"What were the windows like?"

Freddie closed her eyes and pictured the room. The first part of their plan had been for her to get within to see what they were dealing with. Then they would determine how best to release Miles.

"They were locked, of course, but I believe there were bars across them, with padlocks."

"Would it be possible for a person to slip through the bars?"

Freddie hesitated, nibbling her lip. "I could maybe fit through them. I do not think Miles could."

"Very well," the duke said, steepling his fingers together in front of his face, "and the door?"

"There were multiple locks," Freddie said, remembering. "But they were all from the outside. Two of them required keys."

"Who was within?" Benjamin asked.

"Two doctors — one in particular who seemed more of a threat. And the two sizeable men who were there when Miles was taken." Freddie took a deep, shaky breath as she attempted to calm herself as panic began to rise within her once more.

"Anyone else?" the duke asked. "What about staff? Were there many about?"

Freddie closed her eyes. She had been so distraught about Miles' entire plight that she had not been nearly as observant as usual, but fortunately, she noticed more than most people did.

"A butler allowed me entrance," she said, concentrating. "I believe I saw a couple of maids. That is all I can recall."

Benjamin nodded. "I only remember visiting this estate once before. There is not likely a large staff. They are employed by my father, but I am not entirely sure whether or not they would be faithful to him."

"There is something else," Freddie said, hesitantly. She didn't want to share Miles' deepest thoughts with everyone, but they had come this far and they deserved to know. "I am not entirely sure Miles *wants* to be rescued. He kept saying strange things about me living my life and finding another and about how he wanted me to be happy without him."

Benjamin crossed his arms over his chest. "He thinks my father is going to have him killed and he doesn't want you to be caught up in it all, most likely."

"Foolish man," Freddie muttered, and Benjamin shrugged. "He can be."

A sound caught Freddie's attention, and she cocked her ear. "Do you hear that?" She asked the others. "It sounds like—"

"Horse's hooves. And a carriage," finished Jemima, and they all peered through the trees to see a carriage coming down the road toward the estate.

"It's my father's," Benjamin said grimly, and Freddie stared at him in horror.

"Benjamin, that could mean—"

"I know."

"We have to act fast," Freddie said. She took a moment to sit on a fallen log, place her hands at her temples, and breathe. Miles had told her that she always felt she had to fix every situation. Well, he was, in fact, right, and this, she was going to fix. She had to.

"Rebecca, do you have your sketchpad?" she asked.

"I do."

"Benjamin, can you remember the layout of the estate?"

"Somewhat."

"All right," Freddie said, standing and taking command now as a plan began to formulate in her mind. "Between me and Benjamin, we will describe the estate as best we can, if you can quickly — very quickly — sketch it out, Rebecca. Then, I have a few ideas." She looked around at the lot of them. "If any of you do not feel comfortable with this, then you can stay here and I will think nothing of it. But if you are in now, you must remain in. What do you think?"

They all looked at her without a glimmer of hesitation.

"Of course," Celeste said with a smile and a warm voice as she placed her hand on Freddie's shoulder. "We're here for you."

"Excellent," Freddie said with a wobbly smile. "Now, here is what we are going to do."

* * *

A SHORT TIME LATER, they watched Celeste walk up to the servant's entrance. Of all of them, she was the least likely to be recognized, and she assured them she could fool anyone who questioned her.

Much relied on Celeste's success — that, and timing. If Celeste took too long, or if they continued on with their next step too early… then they were in trouble.

After she left, the rest of them needed to cross the yard to the wall of the estate. Freddie was fairly sure which window belonged to the room where Miles was being held. Once they were close, she was sure she would know it by the bars on the window. She was right. After the six of them made their way behind shrubbery for as long as they were able, they hurried across the field, not wanting to risk being caught out in the open for too long. They made it to the wall of the manor without hearing anyone call out to them, though all of them but the duke and his valet, Mr. Thompkins, were breathing heavily from their sprint.

"It's up there," Freddie sputtered. "I could see the bars as we ran."

"It's not particularly far up," the duke said, assessing the wall. "The bricks are firm, but there are a few protruding. Could you use them as a foothold if we helped you?"

"Freddie shouldn't be the one climbing," Jemima protested. "What if she fell? What if—"

"There's no other way," the duke cut in. "She's the only one who will fit."

They were all silent for a moment. Freddie took a deep breath and clapped her hands together.

"Well, here we go."

She placed her hands on the outcropping, but couldn't find a close foothold.

"I'll need a boost."

She realized she wasn't exactly in the best attire for climbing and looked back with flushed cheeks. "Er… preferably one of the ladies, perhaps?"

Jemima, the tallest, cupped her hands and held them in front of her to give Freddie a step up onto the brick.

Freddie turned to her in thanks, and Jemima smiled slightly crookedly.

"Good luck," she said, and Freddie nodded as she began to climb.

She had never been the most graceful of women, but she was determined, and in this, she vowed, she would not fail. Brick by brick, step by step, she ignored the scrape of the rough brick upon her hands, refused to look down, and focused only on the window above her. There was a slight ledge beneath it where she could wait until the timing was right to enter the room. Her role was simple — to ensure Miles was prepared to leave, and to provide a distraction long enough to give the rest of them the time they needed. Whether she had to revive him or untie him or remove a straitjacket — she didn't even want to think of what the possibilities might be — once she entered, he must be ready when the duke arrived, in case they needed to make a hasty departure. She could only hope that Celeste would be able to find keys and get them to the duke in time.

She finally made it to the top and eased her way over the ledge, while being poked and prodded by the variety of neglected plants and weeds that had overtaken the planter. A harsh ripping sound told her she now had a tear in her dress as she came to her knees to look through the window above. She placed her fingers on the bars and lifted her head up and over.

The window was locked, but she had a plan for that. She reached into the pocket of her cloak, grateful for the small contraption she had created many years ago. At the time, it had come in handy for picking locks when her sisters attempted to hide from her, gossip, or steal kisses with their beaus. Now she slipped it into the lock of the window, though she was out of practice and had to work hard at the mechanism before it gave within her hands.

Finally, it clicked and she inwardly gave a shout of triumph.

His father was in the room now, and Miles was submerged in a bathtub. His head was exposed, but above him was the second doctor along with the two men and another Freddie took to be a footman, pouring buckets of water over his head. From Miles' shout, audible through the window, as well as the way he was shaking, Freddie imagined it was freezing cold.

Lord Dorrington stood at the entryway, arms crossed over his chest and a grim smile over his face as he watched. The first doctor stood next to him, seemingly quite agitated as he shuffled from one foot to another, his fingers tapping nervously on the side of his leg.

Freddie pushed at the window slowly but firmly so that she could better hear as she prayed for the duke and Mr. Thompkins to hurry. Their original plan to rescue Miles without the knowledge of the marquess was likely not going to work. They were going to have to force their way out. She hoped the men were ready.

"That's enough," Lord Dorrington said. "Wouldn't want to

kill Lord Gilmore, now would we? Bring him out. Give him something to let him sleep."

"How deep of a sleep would you like, Lord Dorrington?" the doctor in charge asked, and Lord Dorrington only nodded in response, confusing Freddie. Then he shared a look of understanding with the doctor.

"Put him into a deep sleep, Doctor Gibbons," he said with a pointed finger. "A very deep sleep."

"Are you sure, my lord?" he asked as the other men lifted Miles out of the tub and helped him to dress once more.

"Very sure, Doctor Gibbons," Lord Dorrington said with a nod. "It is time."

Doctor Gibbons crossed the room and picked up a bottle that Freddie assumed was laudanum. He began to pour it into a nearby cup. Despite having little knowledge of the medication, Freddie assumed a spoonful was all that required. Drinking near a cupful? It would kill Miles.

As all in the room seemed to be well aware.

The other doctor finally stepped forward, although with a bit of hesitancy.

"St-stop this," he said, visibly shaking as he faced the rest of them. "I cannot condone this."

"You will do as I pay you to do," Lord Dorrington said. "Besides, Doctor Brown, I believe you agreed to my son's lunacy, did you not?"

"I wasn't aware that—"

"That will be quite enough," Lord Dorrington said. "You wouldn't want this to get out, would you? For you are just as much a part of this as anyone else."

Then Lord Dorrington reached into his jacket and pulled out a small pistol — one that Freddie had seen within many carriages in case of attack.

"Back away, Doctor Brown. Now," he said as he turned to Doctor Gibbons. "Give him the drink."

"No!" Doctor Brown said, but he didn't have much choice as the two men held Miles down.

Freddie couldn't wait any longer. She squeezed her upper body through the bars and then, in nearly one motion, she pushed the window open and launched herself into the room.

CHAPTER 27

*M*iles was fighting the men — or trying to — but he was so cold from the "water therapy," as Doctor Gibbons called it, that he could hardly move. He had nearly resigned himself to his fate when a flash of color caught his notice out of the corner of his eye.

He nearly died of shock instead of laudanum when he saw that it was his wife sprawled across the floor of the room.

"Devil it, woman!" his father bellowed from across the room, so loudly that even Miles could hear him. "Will you not give up?"

"Never!" Freddie said fiercely, and despite his chagrin at seeing her here, standing up to these men who would likely kill her for her presence, Miles had never loved her more. "I will never stand idly by and allow you to attempt to kill my husband, who has done nothing but be true to the man he is — the man born to you. We will go — leave England, and never return — if you will only give us leave."

"And then what? You will return upon my death?" Lord Dorrington said with a snort. "I think not."

197

He lifted his pistol. "Move aside, Lady Gilmore."

The men holding Miles had loosened their grip upon Freddie's entrance, and now, mesmerized by the scene in front of them, appeared to have all but forgotten him. Miles took advantage of their momentary lapse in attention and surged forward out of their grasp to stand in front of Freddie.

"Put the pistol down, Father," he said calmly, but his father simply sneered at him.

"Now why do you suppose I would do such a thing?" he asked. "I have three men here who will back me, Miles. You can barely stand — yes, I can tell how weak you are. How weak you have always been. Move away from your wife. Tell her to leave, and this time, to not return. Otherwise, she will suffer the same fate as you."

"Are you sure you should let her go?" Doctor Gibbons asked with worry. "She could tell of what happened here."

"And what did happen here?" Lord Dorrington said, lifting an eyebrow. "We were simply treating the madness of my son, and a miscalculation was made during treatment. It was no one's fault. He was too far gone. Besides, no one would ever believe a woman in the throes of grief over the word of a marquess."

The door suddenly burst open.

"Perhaps not. But would they believe the man who would become the marquess' heir as a result?"

"Or a duke?"

Relief rushed through Miles at the two men — no, make that three — standing in the doorway. His brother entered first, agony crossing his face at the scene he encountered. Beside him stood the Duke of Wyndham. A third man was just behind, one Miles didn't recognize. But he was clearly there to help him, so it didn't much matter who he was.

"Benjamin!" his father exclaimed, unease crossing his face

for the first time since he had entered the room. "What are you doing here? How did you get in?"

Benjamin held up a set of keys.

"With these," he said, placing them in his pocket. "What do you think you are doing, Father?"

"How long have you been here?" his father asked instead, but Benjamin just shook his head.

"Long enough," he said with a sigh. "Long enough to hear what you intended to do with Miles, though it has been apparent for some time now. How could you?"

"Benjamin," his father hissed. "Listen to yourself. You are being ridiculous. I have raised you better than this."

"Fortunately, Father, you were not there much during my childhood," Benjamin said with a wry smile. "Instead, I had a mother who showed us what love and care meant. Who taught us to always be there for one another. It just took someone" —he looked at Freddie with a smile— "to remind me that sometimes love means going to great lengths, beyond what one would ever have imagined. So here we are. Put the gun away, Father, and let us take Miles away from here."

Wildness filled his father's eyes, as he looked from the doorway to Miles and Freddie, then back to the door.

"Leave, Benjamin, and take your friends with you," he said, waving the pistol desperately, and Miles shoved Freddie firmly behind him.

"Don't do this, Father," Benjamin said, as the duke began to take slow steps toward Lord Dorrington.

"I am the one in charge!" his father said, his face taking on an almost manic glow. "You will all do as *I* please! Men, take the interlopers!" he ordered as he began to advance on Miles.

The two brutes rushed toward the duke and his friend, but Miles wasn't considerably worried. He recalled that the duke was renowned for his fists, and had created quite a reputation for himself at Jackson's. He was actually still undefeated — a ridiculous fact to be considering when one's life was at risk, but there it was.

The duke inched ever closer, but Miles braced himself when he saw his father's eyes narrow. Time seemed to slow down as his finger began to tighten on the trigger — and then all sped up again as Benjamin launched himself toward his father and a shot rang out through the room.

The scuffle at the doorway ceased as one of the men went down and the second wobbled unsteadily. One final jab from the duke had him falling on the floor next to his friend.

But it was the scene in front of him that transfixed Miles.

"Benjamin?" he said softly, ensuring his brother was well, and Benjamin answered with a slow nod, his gaze fixed on the floor in front of him.

Miles joined him, standing next to him, noticing with the back of his mind that Freddie had eased in beside him, placing her hand on his arm.

They all stood there, staring down at the marquess. He lay on his back, his eyes wide as he stared up at them. His mouth worked, but nothing came out. A small dribble of blood leaked from the corner of his mouth, his hands clutching his stomach.

The doctors rushed over and began to treat the wound, but Miles and Benjamin shared a look. A gunshot through the stomach was not likely something their father was going to survive. Miles didn't feel any sense of grief, but rather shock that after everything this could be the end. While their father was a despicable man, they couldn't leave him to die.

With the doctors, they lifted him to the bed, told the men to give him the best treatment possible, and then left the room with the rest of the occupants. The duke and his friend — Thompkins, Miles thought he had been called — dragged the two men out with them.

They all stood in shocked silence outside the door.

"Let's go downstairs," Benjamin finally said. "Find ourselves something to drink."

Freddie slipped her hand through Miles' arm, helping to steady him as they went down the stairs. He didn't know what to say to her, but he was grateful she was there. Despite his surge of strength in the room, he was beginning to feel rather unsteady on his feet and it helped to have her physical support. She was a small package of power. He had known she was unstoppable but after today... he would never underestimate her again. Or doubt her love. Miles would never have believed someone could have loved him this much.

"You're something of a cat," he mused aloud, and she turned to look at him with confusion.

"A cat?" she asked with bemusement. "I am far from graceful, Miles."

"No matter how many times you are kicked out, you return, again and again."

"Oh," she said with an embarrassed laugh. "I suppose." Then she turned to look at him before they descended the stairwell. "Lucky you."

Despite himself, Miles let out a low guffaw as they mercifully made it downstairs. They had just reached the bottom when the butler and housekeeper rushed toward them from wherever they had been hiding away. They seemed visibly relieved at Miles' presence.

"Lord Miles! Oh, my apologies, Lord Gilmore," the thin, mustached butler said with a quick nod. Miles hadn't seen him since he was a child, remembered his name being Tiller or something of the sort, but recalled he had always been kind to him when others had not been. "I am... pleased to see you about the house, my lord," he said, though relief was clearly much more his emotion.

Miles smiled at the man, who had obviously been perturbed by all that was happening under the roof he had called home for so many years, though unable to do anything about it as it had been directed by the master of the house.

"My father has been shot, Tiller," he said, as the man's face turned into one of shock. "He is upstairs with the doctors. It was an accident," he emphasized. "Can you send up some of the servants to assist them?"

"Of course, of course," he said, noting that the other guests were seated in the parlor before hurrying away while Miles sank into the sofa, his eyes closing of their own accord.

He could dimly hear Freddie speaking, but Miles had no idea just what she was saying. Likely seeing to the other guests Tiller had noted, though who they were, he had no idea. A short time later, however, he was brought back to his senses by the scent of cinnamon and honey, and he found a tray of simple fare before him.

"Eat," Freddie commanded, and he nodded in agreement, accepting the hot tea from her hands and sipping before taking the plate from her as well. She was right. He needed his strength. He had a feeling there would be much misery to come.

He looked over at Freddie's concerned face.

And much joy too, with Freddie in his life. He sighed as he took another bite. Whatever was coming, they could conquer it together. He was sure of it.

They were all silent for a moment, apparently on edge after all that occurred along with the knowledge that the marquess was upstairs, fighting for his life. Miles had no particular feeling about what happened to his father. Of course, his life would be easier without him. But he didn't wish his father dead. He couldn't. He was still his father, and despite what he had done to him, Miles would rather that he found his end by natural means.

He looked over at his brother, who had turned a sickly shade of green.

"It will be all right, Benjamin," he said, but Benjamin shook his head before sinking both hands into his hair. He remained bent over and continued to speak into his hands, leaving Miles to look to Freddie to know what he said.

She reached across Miles to place a hand on Benjamin's shoulder.

"You cannot blame yourself," she said reassuringly. "You couldn't have known that your father would go to such lengths, and it was certainly not your fault that he ended up shooting himself. Had you not tackled him, it would have been Miles on the receiving end of the bullet. He brought this on himself."

"I know," Benjamin said, leaning his elbows on his thighs. "But I should have known this was coming. He's the mad one," he said, looking at Miles. "He was becoming less sane every day, more fanatical about our bloodline. I should have done something about it."

"We can all blame ourselves," Miles said. "But instead we need to move on — depending on what happens now."

Miles saw all of the faces turn to the door of the drawing room, and he followed them to see Doctor Brown standing at the door.

Blood covered the front of his clothing, and he looked at them grimly.

"Lord Dorrington has passed on," he said, looking to Miles. "You, my lord, are the new marquess."

CHAPTER 28

*I*f there was one fortunate bit about the entire sordid plan orchestrated by Lord Dorrington — the *former* Lord Dorrington — it was that he had been so concerned of the family's reputation that he had not allowed word of his son's apparent madness to reach the ears of any in the *ton*. It seemed that instead, he had planned to wait until his son's shocking death and blame it on an illness before naming Benjamin his heir – or so Doctor Brown had told them.

It had been a long, trying day after they had all piled into the carriages and departed for London. They could have stayed the night, but Miles, Benjamin, and Freddie had all been happy to leave the place behind.

"I think we shall have to sell that estate," Miles had said as they bid it adieu and made for home, to which Freddie agreed. He had been slightly sick about taking his father's carriage home, but there were far too many of them to pile into one.

Freddie had hardly been able to keep from launching herself across the carriage and into Miles' arms. As it was, she had kept a tight grip on his hand, vowing that she would never again let him go.

When they reached London, they had stopped first at Dorrington House, where they had explained all to Lady Dorrington, who took the information stoically before lying down once more. They left her in the care of Benjamin before continuing on to their own home, where they had fallen into an exhausted sleep in one another's arms.

Now, Freddie stood in front of the window watching the sun climb over the spread of houses stretching out in front of them before it blanketed the green in its light. Freddie pulled a blanket tightly around her shoulders as she considered how different this morning could have been.

She was filled with Miles' scent as he stepped behind her and wrapped his arms around her, pulling her back against his chest in his embrace.

"Good morning," he whispered in her ear, and she placed her hands over his in response. "Have I told you, Freddie, just how much I love you?"

She turned with a cheeky smile. "Is this what you say to all of the women who climb up a brick wall to rescue you?"

He grimaced. "Please don't remind me of the danger you put yourself in. You should have left me."

"Would you have left me?"

"Never."

"Well, then." She leaned up on her tiptoes. "I love you too, Miles, as you already know."

He placed his hands on her shoulders to look her in the eye. "I have something for you."

"For me?"

"Yes," he said, turning and walking over to the vanity across the room. He picked up a sheaf of papers and returned to her. "These came while we were... away. I had Bartleby bring them up this morning."

"You were awake already?" she asked. She had thought she'd risen before him.

"I couldn't sleep," he said, which was more than understandable. Somehow, however, he seemed quite alert. He shook the papers in his hand. "Don't you want to know what these are?"

"Of course I do," she said, not wanting to admit how much the curiosity was eating away at her. "I was simply seeing after your wellbeing this morning." She held out her hand. "Now give those here."

"Quite demanding, aren't we?" he said, raising an eyebrow, lifting the papers higher, over her head and out of reach. "It's a shame, dear wife, that you are not a bit taller."

"You boor!" she said laughingly as she jumped up to try and catch them. When she missed, she fell against him, and he wrapped an arm around her, drawing her in close.

"You can have them — on one condition," he said.

"Which is?"

"A kiss."

"Oh, very well," she sighed dramatically, leaning in to press her lips upon his, firmly but quickly. There would be time for that later — after she knew what was in the contents of the papers in his hand.

He lowered his hand. "Here you are."

She took the papers from him, slightly confused as her eyes flew over the words. "It's a patent letter," she said wonderingly, "for my urn which cooks the eggs in the steam."

"Yes," he said, a smile on his face. "I took the liberty of naming it. It is now a tea-and-egger."

"Oh," she said, her own smile beginning to grow. "And this is another patent, for my lock-picking device."

"The one that came in so handy yesterday."

"And this…" she said, looking up at him with wide eyes,

"for my candlestick. I didn't even show you that it was working."

"I know," he said, looking endearingly bashful. "I didn't want to interrupt you, nor pester you with questions while you were trying to make it work. I was worried my father deterred you, but I should have known that nothing would stop you. I submitted the papers knowing that you were going to figure it out. You just have to update and re-submit the design."

"I can't believe you did this," she said, clutching the papers to her chest.

"You told me that working on your inventions was a hobby, but I know it is more than that, Freddie. You are passionate about your work, and you should be proud of it too. There should never be the option for another to take any credit for your ideas, and it should be on record that you were the one whose genius led to these innovations."

"Thank you, Miles," she said, placing the papers down next to her. "I am, however, going to need your help with submitting one more."

"One more patent?"

"Yes, exactly," she said, taking his hand. "Come with me."

"We're in our nightclothes!" he protested, and she laughed at him.

"Here, then, don your wrapper," she said, finding it in the dressing room and throwing it at him. He caught it and wrapped it around himself as she did the same with her own. She took his hand and led him out of the room, down the stairwell, and into her workspace.

"I didn't know you were working on something else," he said, and she turned and smiled at him.

"That's because I didn't want you to know."

"Interesting," he murmured.

She hesitated for a moment once they entered the workspace. She turned to him, taking his hands in hers, squeezing them as she looked up at him, imploring him to understand where she was coming from and why she had done what she had.

"The truth is, Miles, you do already know what I was working on. When you found out, you were not exactly pleased, and I understand why. I thought of being rid of the idea altogether, but then... then I began to think more about it, and even if you choose not to use this, there may be others who could benefit from it, so I continued on. I do not want you to think there is anything wrong with the way you are now. I just thought that, particularly when you are somewhere like in the House of Lords, this would be of some assistance."

She released his hands and rounded the back of her workspace, finding what she was looking for.

"Here it is," she said, holding in her hands the design she was most proud of. "I call it – very unoriginally – a trumpet headband. I based it off of the ear trumpet but attempted to make it a bit more inconspicuous. It also allows you the use of both hands while wearing it. You can wear it around your neck or over your head. I hope it fits. I tried to size your head as best I could without you noticing."

She held it out toward him timidly, unsure of what his reaction would be. Miles was a difficult man to read most days. He had been insulted before when he had thought she was trying to "fix" him. Would he understand that she was just trying to help?

He took a step toward her, then reached out and took the device from her. Slowly, he put it around his head. She reached up and helped him fit the trumpets underneath his ears.

"Say something, please," he said, and she nodded.

"I love you, Miles."

His lips sprang into a smile.

"I could hear that," he said, wonder filling his widened eyes. "Perhaps not as well as you might hear everything around you, but much better than usual."

"Are they comfortable?" she asked, hope springing within her breast.

"They're not terrible," he said, to which she laughed.

"That's a ringing endorsement."

"Freddie," he said, holding out his hands to her. "Thank you."

"You're welcome."

"I am sorry if I doubted you before. It was my own fault, but I allowed my father to get into my head, to question your motives, which I never should have done. For you, Freddie, are the kindest, most giving person I have ever met. I realize now that it is not so much that you want to fix everything, but more so that you want to help everyone you meet, in whatever way you can. Even more admirable is the fact that you are perfectly capable of doing whatever you put your mind to. Your intelligence is admirable. And you know something?"

"What's that?" she tilted her head, her heart swelling at his words.

"I'd like to ask you to marry me, but I have already done so," he said, grinning. "But I must tell you that I love you more than I ever could have believed was possible. Thank you for all you have given me."

"You're very welcome," she said, answering his smile with one of her own. "That was quite a speech."

"It was, wasn't it?" he said with a laugh.

"I believe those were more words than all the rest you have ever said to me since we were married."

"That just may be so," he said ruefully. "Are you still glad you married me? You wanted a man who would leave you alone. Well, my dear, unfortunately that will not be the case. For it seems I cannot keep my hands off of you."

"I am more than glad I married you," she said, raising an eyebrow. "And my opinion has changed. I no longer wish for you to leave me alone. In fact," she reached up and gripped the lapels of his wrapper, "I would very much like your full, undivided attention."

"For that, I think we are going to have to go back upstairs," he said, and before she knew what he was doing, he reached down, wrapped an arm around the backs of her knees, and scooped her up off her feet.

"Miles!" she cried, "What are you doing?"

"I am carrying my bride upstairs, just as I should have done the day we were married." He shook his head as he walked down the corridor. "What a fool I was. Think of all those days and nights, completely wasted, as I sat in the next room, pining for you but too afraid to go to you."

"Why were you afraid?" she asked softly.

"I was afraid I would lose my heart."

Freddie swallowed the lump that had grown in her throat. "And now?"

"I do not consider it lost. It is more so that you have found it."

"Oh, Miles," she said, tilting her head back to look up at him dreamily. "That was ever so romantic."

"Good, for I meant it that way," he said, huffing ever so slightly as he crested the final stair and continued down the upstairs corridor. They startled a maid who was coming out of one of the bedrooms, but her look of shock turned into a smile before she scurried down the hall and back downstairs.

Miles finally set Freddie down on the bed, and she sank into the coverlet before reaching out and pulling Miles down with her. He came eagerly, sinking his hands into her long, unbound hair. The early morning rays of the sun filtered in through the bedroom window, causing his eyes to gleam nearly gold.

Freddie awaited his kiss, but he paused for a moment, smiled wickedly at her as though he was planning something devious, and then he leaned down the rest of the way and pressed his lips against hers. She opened her mouth to him, and when their tongues tangled and he gently bit down on her lower lip, desire coursed through her. Would she ever stop having this insatiable longing for her husband? She hoped not.

He seemed to feel the same sense of togetherness, for he left her mouth for a moment to rain kisses over her nose, her cheeks, her forehead, and finally down her neck before he trailed them lower, ending on her collarbone.

He worked the sleeves of her wrapper down her arms, and she helped him by pulling them free. Finally, he lifted her night rail over her head, leaving her bare before him. Freddie paused, snuggling down underneath the blankets, tugging at Miles' hand for him to follow her.

"Cold?" he asked, and she nodded. He dispensed with his own nightclothes before joining her, skimming his hands up and down her sides.

Freddie was torn between the notion of wanting to lie there for the rest of the day as he teased her, and waiting for him to come home and bring her to fulfillment.

Finally, he settled himself between her thighs and thrust deep, causing Freddie to cry out as she sunk her hands into his hair.

He kissed her once more, whispering her name on her lips as he found his fulfillment at nearly the same time as she.

When Freddie finally opened her eyes to look at him, she couldn't help but smile.

"You kept your trumpets on."

"I did." He grinned wickedly. "The better to hear you, my dear."

"Oh my," she said, her cheeks heating slightly. "What did you think?"

"I think I like the way these amplify sound," he said, reaching an arm out to pull her close. "And you, my love, make much noise."

"Miles!"

"You are *quite* the snorer. Even I could often hear you as it was. Now with these…" he laughed, "I am beginning to wonder if these were a good idea, for I shall now be able to hear you all of the time that you are speaking, which is quite often."

"Compared to you!" she exclaimed, but he laughed.

"I'm joking," he said. "I like hearing you talk."

"Good," she said, raising her nose in the air, "for you have many more years of it."

"Well, with this fine start to the day," he said, "are you ready to face the rest of it?"

"Yes," she said. "Anything, with you."

"Good," he said, before looking her up and down and smiling wickedly. "For I have just the idea. There is this something I have been longing to paint…"

EPILOGUE

*M*iles wasn't even through the doorway when he was practically accosted by Freddie.

"Did you do it? What did they say? Is there support? When will changes be made?"

Her words came so rapidly that had he not known her better, he likely would have missed half of it. But with the trumpet headband, he picked up most of what he hadn't read on her expressive lips — lips he now leaned over to kiss.

"I suggested it, yes," he said. "But these things take time, Freddie. Now it is a matter of waiting until a bill is proposed."

"But how could they not?" she said. "The conditions of so many people — whether they are, in truth, sane or not — are at stake. Why, even now, they are likely suffering."

"I know," Miles said, reaching out to take her in her arms. "I love how much your heart bleeds for others, Freddie. I promise I am doing all that I can to fix things. We have to trust the process."

"This is why I enjoy working alone," she grumbled, and he laughed.

"You can't do everything alone," he said with a wink, and her mouth opened in surprise.

"Miles!" she exclaimed. "You are becoming rather cheeky."

"My wife is a bad influence," he laughed as he followed her through the house to the drawing room. They had decided not to move to Dorrington House. He had assumed his father's place and the responsibility in every other way, but his mother and Benjamin had kept the house.

Freddie continued to remind him that this was a new beginning, a change he must embrace.

For all of his life, Miles had been dreading becoming the marquess. He had been unsure of whether or not he would be able to take on all that the role demanded. But, it seemed, he was much more adept at it than he had thought. He enjoyed managing the estates, and he was looking forward to spending the recess from Parliament visiting each of them before he and Freddie would settle in their country home for the remainder of the year.

He wished he had joined the House of Lords sooner. While his one complaint would be that the pace moved either too rapidly or too slowly, it was enjoyable to put his thoughts and experiences to good use, to do what he could to make a difference in England. He would try to prove his worth.

As for his certificate of madness...

"I have more news," he said, as he found his spirits in the cabinet and poured himself a drink. "After Doctor Brown reversed the certification of lunacy and testified as to the actions of Doctor Gibbons, Doctor Gibbons has been banned from providing any more treatments to mentally unsound patients — or those who are claimed to be." Miles sighed deeply. "I'm afraid that reform for the mentally ill will be a long time coming, Freddie," he said. "There are little things that can be done. If someone is found to be ill-treating patients, there are always repercussions, of course. But these false accusations... I was one of the lucky ones."

"That you were," she agreed. "I have been trying to convince other women to join with me to provide visits and care to the mentally ill just as many do with the hospitals, but it is difficult. Many are nervous."

"Understandably so," he said, nodding. He placed his drink on the table and held out an arm to her. "Come sit."

She dutifully walked over, though there was a glint in her eye that told him she wasn't particularly pleased with being told what to do. She perched on his thigh and then leaned in against his chest.

"What did you do today?"

"My friends were here," she said. "Celeste was telling us all about a discovery she is hoping to make. I cannot say I quite understood what she was saying, but I hope she is successful."

He wrapped his arm around her and twined her fingers within his.

"Tell me what these hands have created today."

"Nothing yet."

"What are they working on?"

"A device that will rock a cradle without anyone having to be there to do so."

"How would you do that?"

"Well, I was thinking that—"

"Wait." He suddenly registered her words. "Why are you working on such a thing?"

"Well," she said, sitting up and turning so that she was looking at him. A smile stretched across her face from one ear to the other. "I thought we might need it."

He swallowed hard. "Will we?"

"Yes," she said nodding, tears springing to her eyes as she laughed, "for when the baby comes."

Miles found that suddenly he had lost the ability to speak altogether. It didn't matter, though, for he could say all he needed to with his actions instead. He fiercely pulled Freddie toward him, wrapping her tightly in an embrace.

"Miles," she said in his ear.

"Yes?"

"You're squeezing me a little tight."

He instantly let go, holding her out in front of him.

"Did I hurt you? Did I hurt the baby? Oh, Freddie, I—"

She held out a hand, laughing. "I'm fine. The baby's fine. All will be well."

"Good," he said. "And it will be well, because I promise you, Freddie, I will be the one protecting you. Anything you need, you will have it. You have only to ask."

"I already know that," she said, bringing her hand to cup his cheek. "I have all that I want, Miles, for I have you. So will this baby. We will be luckier than anyone in the world with you there for us."

"You've invented many amazing things, Freddie, my love," he said, leaning close, resting his forehead upon hers, "but I have a feeling that this will be your best creation yet."

She smiled and kissed him. "You know why?"

"Why is that?"

"Because we did it together."

With a kiss, they confirmed all they shared, all they loved about one another — and, like their life together thus far had proven, the kiss said enough.

No words were needed.

* * *

Dear reader,

Thank you for reading Freddie and Miles' story! I so hope you enjoyed it.

If you're wondering what will happen to Celeste, read on for a preview of her story as she gets involved with a rival astronomer. Or you can go directly to download her story here.

While Freddie is, of course, a completely fictional character, I must note that much of her work and inventions are, in actuality, contributed to Mrs. Sarah Guppy.

Mrs. Guppy lived from 1770 to 1852 – so a little bit ahead of Freddie's time. In 1811, she patented a method to make safe piling for bridges. Her design was used in suspension bridge foundations. From there, she offered technical advice regarding bridges, foundations, and embankments.

In total, ten patents were taken out by her family within the first fifty years of the nineteenth century. Her inventions included a bed with built-in exercise equipment (which Freddie makes mention of in Designs on a Duke), as well as the urn which also cooked eggs, a fire hood, and the new type of candlestick which Freddie invents. In addition, she also created a method to keep ships free from barnacles and a device which improved caulking ships, boats, and other vessels.

The lock pick and ear trumpets Freddie creates are not inspired by Mrs. Guppy, but rather by other inventions at the time.

This entire series is inspired by women like Mrs. Guppy, who were ahead of their time and able to overcome restraints placed on their gender, such as less education than men, in order to further advancements in their fields.

If you haven't yet signed up for my newsletter, I would love to have you join us! You will receive Unmasking a Duke for free, as well as links to giveaways, sales, new releases, and stories about my coffee addiction, my struggle to keep my plants alive, and how much trouble one loveable wolf-looka-like dog can get into.

www.elliestclair.com/ellies-newsletter

Or you can join my Facebook group, Ellie St. Clair's Ever Afters, and stay in touch daily.

Until next time, happy reading!

With love,
Ellie

* * *

Discovering the Baron
The Bluestocking Scandals Book Three

SHE'S SPYING ON HIM. He's engaged to another. Can their stars ever align?

Astronomer Celeste Keswick spends her nights staring at the sky, attempting to discover the planet she knows is out there but cannot yet see. Her brother is convinced that there is one way to do it – for Celeste to spy on the one other man who might find it first. Little does Celeste know what else he will awaken within her.

Lord Oliver Cunningham may be a baron, but all he really wants is the opportunity to study the stars and discover their secrets. Aware that the time has come to marry and produce heirs, he finally agrees to an arranged marriage -- a decision he will soon regret, for his new assistant is far more than she seems.

In the race to uncover the next astronomical discovery, Celeste must choose whether to give her loyalty to her brother or the man she is falling for – the very man she cannot have. For Oliver can't decide what is worse – having to see Celeste every day with the knowledge he should not touch her, or the thought of spending the rest of his life without her.

Can Celeste and Oliver overcome all that stands between them to find the planet they are searching for and the love they never knew they needed?

AN EXCERPT FROM
DISCOVERING THE BARON

*C*eleste was grateful for one thing — she knew this house well enough to be entirely aware of just where the exits were through which she could escape. The Duke and Duchess of Wyndham lived in one of the largest mansions in London — it could hardly be called a house, in her viewpoint.

She had snuck out of the ballroom through the parlor until she came to what most would call a conservatory, although she knew better. Her dearest friend Jemima, sister to the duke, had a laboratory hidden away in the corner of the large room, although tonight the vegetation was artfully arranged so that any who came this way would not stumble upon the secret that Jemima was much more than a beautiful woman — though that she was as well.

But her friend's laboratory was not Celeste's destination. No, hers was beyond this room. She pushed through the garden doors, her feet in their kid slippers padding over the stone to the low balcony railing to overlook the rolling green beyond. The duke's mother had insisted that when the house was completed, so were the gardens, for they would be the envy of all who saw them. Rebecca, the duke's wife and the architect of the home, had complied.

It was beautiful out here, of course, but Celeste was not entirely interested in the small fountains and lush florals stretching out below her.

Instead, she turned around, leaned back against the railing, and looked up at the stars far above her, sighing with relief.

Out here she found peace. The ballroom was loud, noisy, crowded, and she had spent long enough hiding in a corner with Jemima. She had seen her mother look her way, her expression changing to the calculating one that told Celeste she was determined to see her daughter upon the arm of a man with "Lord" in front of his name. Thus, Celeste had gone running, leaving Jemima laughing behind her.

She let her gaze wander upon the sky above, searching out the stars that had always called to her, that were home for her. She ignored the cold stone of the balcony upon her back as she lifted a finger, tracing the pattern of the constellation.

"Is there a shooting star tonight?"

As Celeste tried to right herself in order to see who had disturbed her sanctuary, her feet got caught in her skirts, and she scrambled to catch hold of the balcony in order to hold herself up. Instead, however, she began to topple over backwards, and she let out a noise that could only be described as part-frustrated growl and part-scream as she tried to remember just how far away the ground was below the balcony.

Luckily, it was rather close. As she tumbled, warm fingers brushed against her ankle — goodness, her mother would have a fit if she knew her daughter's uncovered ankles had been flying through the air — but nevertheless she had pitched over backwards.

She was still staring at the stars as she lay on her back, only now it was while lying in a curiously comfortable bed of some unknown greenery.

"Miss Keswick!"

Celeste frowned. She recognized that voice, but from where? Suddenly a face filled her vision, and she was grateful for the darkness of night around them, for she knew that her cheeks were likely filled with a spotted dark red blush — and not the becoming kind.

"Lord Essex!" she exclaimed, attempting to move into a seated position, politely ignoring his outstretched hand, too embarrassed to take it. "How are you this evening?"

How are you this evening? Was she pretending she was greeting him in the midst of the ballroom instead of the middle of the garden where she was unceremoniously attempting to extricate herself from a bed of greenery without tearing her dress or exposing more skin than she already had?

"Miss Keswick, I am so incredibly sorry," he said, finally reaching in and placing his arms around her despite her protestations, which paused as he lifted her out of the flora. He was deceptively strong and smelled divine, his cologne a spicy, heady scent. "I did not mean to startle you, and I certainly should have caught you before you fell."

"Oh, it's entirely my own fault," she finally managed as he righted her. "I should have been paying attention instead of allowing myself to become lost within the sky."

"Within the sky?" he asked, winging up an eyebrow, and Celeste's embarrassment grew.

"It's—nothing. Forget I said anything."

"No, please, Miss Keswick, I would be most interested in learning more of what you were doing."

She looked at him in bemusement, but he wore no smile or mocking look.

"Please?" he repeated, his expression so endearing that she couldn't help but comply.

"Oh, very well," she said, ducking her head. "I was tracing my favorite constellation — well, constellations, for there are actually two of them, although I prefer to see them as one."

"Do you?" he asked, and she nodded. "Tell me of them — of it."

"Perseus and Andromeda," she said, pointing up to the sky. "See the bright star, there? Then follow it around and you will see her. He is on the other side, and the two of them circle the northern hemisphere together."

She looked down at him, seeing he still seemed interested so she continued.

"The legend is that Andromeda's mother, Cassiopeia, boasted that she was the most beautiful woman in the world — even above the gods. So Poseidon, god of the seas and brother of Zeus, who felt his sea nymphs were the most beautiful, created Cetus, a great sea monster, and decreed that Cassiopeia must sacrifice her only daughter, Andromeda, to this terrible beast. Andromeda was chained to a large rock in the sea and left there for it. However, as Cetus approached, Perseus arrived, having just defeated Medusa, whose head he carried in a bag. When Perseus saw the beautiful young woman, he drew the head of Medusa out of the bag. When the sea monster saw it, the creature turned to stone. Perseus then freed Andromeda and took her home as his queen."

She finished the story with a smile on her face, but then made the mistake of looking at Lord Essex, who was staring at her with the strangest of expressions, one she couldn't quite make out. He likely thought her addled, she realized, and she straightened.

"I — ah, forgive me, I shouldn't have rambled like that. In fact, I think I will be returning—"

But she stopped when he reached toward her. For a second, she wondered if he was going to draw her close and kiss her. But instead he plucked something from behind her ear, then held it out between them. "A leaf." He showed her and then let it flutter to the ground. "You look rather like Andromeda tonight."

Celeste was lost for words for a moment as she stared at him. His eyes, the irises so dark that she couldn't determine if they were navy or umber, were crinkled at the corners, his lips turned up in a small smile.

"You knew!" she finally exclaimed. "You knew that entire story."

"I did," he confirmed, his smile widening now. "But I have never heard it told quite like you just did, with such wonder and emotion. I knew you were a woman of science, Miss Keswick, but I never realized you were a romantic as well."

"Oh!" she said, covering her mouth with her hand. "I'm not sure that I would be called a romantic. I just... I love the story, as well as the thought that the stars are always with us, wherever we may be."

"True words, Miss Keswick," he said, and she was caught by his eyes once more. Onyx, she decided, that's what they were. She was so lost in their depths, for they were as dark as the night sky. She had spent time in his presence before, but it was always within polite company. He was a handsome man, to be sure — every woman who saw him must think the same — but never had she allowed herself a moment to think that he might hold any attraction or regard for her, and so she had kept herself from such *romantic*, as he put it, thoughts regarding him.

Or anyone, really. She had resigned herself to the fact that she would likely live out her days as had William Herschel's sister, Caroline — known for her work and the assistance she provided her brother, but never finding love for herself.

Celeste's love was the stars above, and her affection would have to be maintained for the family she already had.

For gentlemen were not particularly inclined to be interested in a bluestocking such as she. Any interest they initially showed quickly fled when she opened her mouth about her work or her aspirations. No man desired a wife of science.

Celeste and Jemima had consoled themselves with the thought that, at the very least, they would always have each other.

Romance was for others, or in the pages of the books Celeste allowed herself now and again as an escape.

She shook her head before allowing any thoughts of Lord Essex to intrude. She began to list all of the reasons why he would likely never even want to see her again, let alone harbor any romantic thoughts toward her.

First, he was one of the most handsome, charming gentlemen she had ever met. She hadn't much experience with men of the *ton*, but she assumed he was one that many young women would be interested in. Whereas she… well, she was not exactly the paragon of loveliness. She had bright red hair, freckles that were not merely scattered becomingly across her nose but rather covered her entire face, and a complexion that was near to translucent until she blushed — which was often — and then she turned a shade of red that would make a tomato jealous.

Second, she had met him before, when she had made no blunder whatsoever, and he had clearly been unenamored.

Third, she had just waxed on about the stars and her love of all things celestial. No man of his ilk would think anything of a bluestocking who would prefer to spend her days staring through a metal cylinder or making calculations on pages before her.

Fourth, he was a baron, while she was nothing more than a common woman whose father had made money through importing and exporting. While she was proud of her father for how hard he had worked and for making something of himself, she knew that most within the nobility would think nothing of it.

Fifth and finally (she always thought lists should be in denominations of five), she had just made a fool of herself in front of him. He was likely internally laughing at her and desperate to find a way to extricate himself from this situation.

"Miss Keswick, what are you counting?" he asked, interrupting her thoughts, and she dropped her hands suddenly when she realized she had been counting on her fingers. She fisted her hands into her skirts to keep them hidden from view as her face burned anew.

"Nothing," she said immediately, and he smiled knowingly but didn't press her.

"While I have enjoyed this interlude with you, it would not be seemly for the two of us to be found out here together. I *would* escort you back into the ballroom, but that certainly wouldn't do. So tell me, Miss Keswick, would you like to remain here awhile longer, or would you like to be the first to return?"

Just as she had thought. He was more than eager to be rid of her company.

"I, ah, I shall return and leave you to your own time alone," she said hurriedly. "I needed a moment away from it all, and I have been out here long enough. My mother will be positively livid that I— I'm sorry, you likely have no care for all of that."

"Nothing to apologize for, Miss Keswick," he said. "I enjoy listening to you talk."

He was being polite. He had to be. No one enjoyed listening to her talk. Even her friends, who allowed her to go off on her tangents, watched her with courteous smiles on their faces until she remembered herself and the fact that they had no interest in how to calculate the distance between stars or the speed of a comet.

"Goodbye, then, Lord Essex."

"Goodbye, Miss Keswick."

* * *

KEEP READING *DISCOVERING the Baron* here!

ALSO BY ELLIE ST. CLAIR

A Time to Love

A Time to Dream

Thieves of Desire

The Art of Stealing a Duke's Heart

A Jewel for the Taking

A Prize Worth Fighting For

Gambling for the Lost Lord's Love

Romance of a Robbery

Blooming Brides

A Duke for Daisy

A Marquess for Marigold

An Earl for Iris

A Viscount for Violet

The Blooming Brides Box Set: Books 1-4

Happily Ever After

The Duke She Wished For

Someday Her Duke Will Come

Once Upon a Duke's Dream

He's a Duke, But I Love Him

Loved by the Viscount

Because the Earl Loved Me

Happily Ever After Box Set Books 1-3

Happily Ever After Box Set Books 4-6

The Victorian Highlanders

Duncan's Christmas - (prequel)

Callum's Vow

Finlay's Duty

Adam's Call

Roderick's Purpose

Peggy's Love

The Victorian Highlanders Box Set Books 1-5

Searching Hearts

Duke of Christmas (prequel)

Quest of Honor

Clue of Affection

Hearts of Trust

Hope of Romance

Promise of Redemption

Searching Hearts Box Set (Books 1-5)

Standalones

Always Your Love

The Stormswept Stowaway

A Touch of Temptation

Christmastide with His Countess

Her Christmas Wish

Merry Misrule

A Match Made at Christmas

For a full list of all of Ellie's books, please see

www.elliestclair.com/books.

ABOUT THE AUTHOR

Ellie has always loved reading, writing, and history. For many years she has written short stories, non-fiction, and has worked on her true love and passion -- romance novels.

In every era there is the chance for romance, and Ellie enjoys exploring many different time periods, cultures, and geographic locations. No matter when or where, love can always prevail. She has a particular soft spot for the bad boys of history, and loves a strong heroine in her stories.

Ellie and her husband love nothing more than spending time at home with their children and Husky cross. Ellie can typically be found at the lake in the summer, pushing the stroller all year round, and, of course, with her computer in her lap or a book in hand.

She also loves corresponding with readers, so be sure to contact her!

www.elliestclair.com
ellie@elliestclair.com

Printed in Great Britain
by Amazon

57803795R00138